the Wish List

The Worst Fairy Godmother Ever!

the Wish List

The Worst Fairy Godmother Ever!

By Sarah Aronson

Scholastic Press

New York

Library of Congress Cataloging-in-Publication Data available

ISBN 978-0-545-94151-8

10 9 8 7 6 5 4 3 2 1   17 18 19 20 21

Printed in the U.S.A   23

First edition, June 2017

Book design by Maeve Norton

For my mom and dad,
the best parents ever!

Chapter One

Sisters!

Dear Trainee, Please read and review all the rules before the first day of training. We appreciate your cooperation. —The Bests

Isabelle didn't have to be told she'd be better off studying.

She knew she wasn't ready for the first day of Fairy Godmother Training: Level One—not by a long shot. She didn't need her older sister, Clotilda, to tell her that.

But that didn't stop Clotilda. All day long, she asked things like: Why aren't you studying? Can I give you a quiz? You didn't fall asleep on your book again, did you?

This was the problem with older, smarter sisters who were perfect at everything. Clotilda wasn't just annoying. She was also right.

"Why can't you take this seriously?" she asked Isabelle. And then the clincher: "You don't want to embarrass Grandmomma, do you?"

Grandmomma (with the emphasis on *grand*) was the current president of the Fairy Godmother Alliance, one of the authors of *The Official Rule Book for Fairy Godmothers, 11th Edition*, and the sisters' grandmother.

More important, Grandmomma ran the official fairy godmother training program and helped select practice princesses for every new trainee. She was a godmother with very high standards and a very short temper. Trainees who couldn't cut it were banished. Probably to the dreaded Fairy Godmother Home for Normal Girls.

Isabelle did not want to go there.

At the Fairy Godmother Home for Normal Girls, there were no princesses. There were no wands. There were definitely no sparkles. Instead, normal girls learned to do one of the non-magical jobs of the fairy godmother world. "It's an honest life," Clotilda had told Isabelle at least a hundred times. "It's nothing to be ashamed of, but let's be honest, being a fairy godmother is so much better."

So, no, Isabelle didn't want to embarrass (or otherwise irritate) Grandmomma. But she didn't want to study, either. The problem with studying was that there was always something better to do.

Like eating cinnamon pies and chocolate twigs and running so fast she could almost fly. Or building puffy cloud castles that floated up into the deep-blue sky. Or going to her secret hiding place near the top of the castle tower. Isabelle always had great ideas when she sat in the cozy space between the girlgoyles (her word for the gargoyles, since they looked like girls). The girlgoyles weren't magical—they never came to life or told jokes or helped her out in any real way—but they didn't nag her, either. Sometimes, when she was feeling extra lonely, she pretended that one of them was her long-lost mother. Even though she was a tiny baby when Mom went away for good, Isabelle felt close to her when she was with the girlgoyles. She missed her all the time. She definitely did not believe what everyone said. Her mother was not the worst fairy godmother ever.

If only Clotilda would leave her alone, she'd go there right now.

But Clotilda would not leave her alone. Not for one second. Not when she could be telling her what to do.

"A great fairy godmother believes in happiness," Clotilda recited. "She knows just what to do when her princess finds herself in an emergency."

That didn't sound so complicated. "Okay," Isabelle said, "go ahead and test me."

Clotilda turned to the first practice quiz at the back of the book. "Question Number One: What must you possess to pass your first level of fairy godmother training?"

Isabelle groaned. These questions! They were never as simple as they seemed. Plus, she could smell gooey pumpkin cakes baking in the kitchen below. Also, a bluebird had landed at the window and was singing a magical song.

"A ton of sparkles? A brand-new wand?" she tried, looking past Clotilda and out to the beautiful sunny day beyond her.

Clotilda pulled the curtains shut. "Isabelle, you should know that no one's going to trust you with more than a teaspoon of sparkles until at least Level Two. Wait for the choices. I bet once you hear them, the right answer will click."

Isabelle hated waiting. She hated the choices, too, because they were always confusing. Most of all, she hated feeling jealous of her sister. Clotilda had passed all four levels of training, as she would say, lickety-split. Or as Grandmomma would say, faster than any new godmother ever, she "couldn't be more proud."

Clotilda was a picture-perfect godmother. She was loving and kind (just not always to her sister), cheerful and smart, and skilled in the fine art of fairy godmother gift-giving. Isabelle had watched her turn a raisin into a sleek black convertible and an old trunk of rags into a fabulous wardrobe. She knew which magical blessings to offer new babies, and when blessings were not enough to ward off evil, she could snap her fingers and put a princess into a long sleep to protect her. Clotilda even *looked* like Isabelle's version of a perfect fairy godmother. She had pretty ears, dainty feet, and shiny long hair. She wound it into a bun in the morning, and it stayed put all day.

Isabelle's hair never stayed put. No matter how many pins she used, it always looked messy.

"I'm sorry," Isabelle said. "Give me the choices."

Clotilda spoke very, very slowly. "It's either a) kindness, b) determination, c) gusto, or d)"—she paused dramatically—"all of the above."

Isabelle liked the sound of the word *gusto*, but she wasn't sure what it meant. "Determination?" she guessed.

Clotilda said nothing.

"Kindness?"

When Clotilda scowled, she looked a lot like Grandmomma. "The right answer is d) all of the above." She started to read Question Number Two, but then she stopped halfway through. "Isabelle, snap to it! Training starts in two days. Don't you care about becoming a great fairy godmother?"

"Yes! I mean, no. I mean, what was the question?" Isabelle hadn't been listening. But that wasn't because she didn't care. The truth was Isabelle cared a lot. She cared more about becoming a fairy godmother than almost anything else in the fairy godmother universe.

She just didn't like tests. There were too many rules.

Every time she opened the rule book she fell asleep.

For Isabelle, the answer to the question "What do you need to pass your first level of training?" was not *all of the above*. It was *none of the above*. She had to be more than

a) kind,

b) determined,

c) full of gusto (whatever that was), and

d) all of the above.

No matter how scary it seemed, she was going to have to e) be brave, f) take some risks, and g) get all of the answers by whatever means possible.

At least, she had to try.

Chapter Two

The Very Dangerous Plan

The next morning, Isabelle woke up extra early. First thing in the morning was the best time to sneak around the castle without getting caught.

Grandmomma was enjoying a long early morning bath. Clotilda was already hard at work, paging through fashion magazines just in case her first real princess, Melody, wished for a new dress. A good fairy godmother had to stay up-to-date!

Isabelle had no time to waste. She slipped past their rooms, climbed two winding staircases, and hurried down the thick red carpet of the hallway to the far back corner of their fairy godmother castle.

In the corner was a very large door.

Besides being very large, it was also very thick and very red and, thanks to a big brass knocker that looked like a lion, somewhat terrifying. It was a door you never knocked on unless you had been summoned. This was the door to Grandmomma's office.

No one was allowed into Grandmomma's office if Grandmomma wasn't there.

But today it was unlocked. This had to be a sign.

With both hands on the matching brass handle, Isabelle pulled as hard as she could. When the door creaked open, she looked left, right, and left again. Seeing that the coast was still clear, she tiptoed into the room and closed the door all the way.

Isabelle tried not to laugh, but it was impossible—
and not just because she was nervous about getting
caught. She laughed because she didn't know where to
look first. There wasn't normally an opportunity to gaze
around Grandmomma's office. Isabelle was usually
too busy getting lectured to do much but stare at the
carpet.

Now she could freely take in all the amazing fairy
godmother bling: pretty jewels and cups and bowls, and
even shoes of all shapes and sizes. The presidents of Wand
Makers Incorporated—as well as Dream-Shoe, Landmark
Castle Repair, and, of course, the Fairy Godmother School
Board—all wanted to stay on Grandmomma's good side,
so they gave her a lot of free stuff.

But even better than the big old spinning wheel in the
middle of the room, there were sparkles. In every corner,
Isabelle saw piles of them! Beautiful, magical, happiness-
making sparkles. Sparkles were the source of all fairy

godmother magic, the ingredient that made wish fulfill-ment possible. She had never seen so many at one time.

Isabelle knew she was not allowed to handle sparkles yet. To be honest, she didn't even know the full extent of their powers. It was probably somewhere in that rule book. But she also knew that forbidden things were · usually the best things. That's why they were forbidden in the first place.

Very carefully, she picked up one sparkle and held it up to the light. When nothing happened, she picked up a few more. And when nothing happened again, she picked up a few more. They looked so beautiful—good enough to eat, even. Cautiously she stuck out her tongue. They tasted like woodchips. Maybe these sparkles were just duds.

There was only one way to find out if they really worked. Isabelle picked up two gigantic handfuls. She took a deep breath and blew as hard as she could.

Right away, the room began to change. "Wow," Isabelle said out loud. She couldn't help herself. It felt like she was standing inside a rainbow! As a few (or more) landed on her, she checked herself out in Grandmomma's vintage mirror. Her messy hair glistened like it was full of diamonds. So did her skin. And her clothes—she couldn't believe it! She looked ready to go to the Extravaganza. Even her nails looked polished. She reached down and threw a few more handfuls into the air. Sparkle magic was going to be a breeze!

The sparkles were so pretty, she didn't worry when her head began to tingle. Or when her arms wanted to shake and her feet felt like dancing. When the room seemed lighter and brighter and almost like it was alive, Isabelle didn't fret. Instead, she thought about grand things. Like passing Level One and going to the Extravaganza. And hugging her mother. Standing there, covered in sparkles, Isabelle could feel deep down that her mother was out there somewhere, waiting to come home.

She had to stop herself from leaping for the chandelier or standing on her head or running right out the door to the top of the tower and the girlgoyles. She could do those things later. It was time to get down to business. She'd come this far and couldn't risk getting caught now.

She sat down at Grandmomma's desk and very carefully opened the top drawer. Isabelle snorted at what she saw. Perfect, put-together Grandmomma was a secret slob!

The drawer was stuffed to the brim with pictures of princesses, and every single one of them was different. There were old faces and young faces of all shapes and sizes, from pale to dark and every shade in between. Some wore lots of fancy makeup. Some wore suits with bow ties and pants. Some wrapped their heads in beautiful scarves or decorated their hair with beads and strings and bows. Some wore all white. Some wore all black. Just like sparkles and snowflakes, there were no two princesses alike.

Except for one thing: All of them were smiling.

All, that is, except one.

The non-smiling girl looked no older than Isabelle. She was wearing jeans. Her hair was a little messy. She looked absolutely miserable.

Isabelle hid the picture at the bottom of the pile. She couldn't help feeling a little sorry for her. The poor girl probably got that way because she had a really mean and bossy older sister.

Isabelle couldn't let herself get distracted. She'd come in here to look for something. She opened the middle drawer.

It was stuffed with candy from every corner of the fairy godmother world. There were chocolate stars, candy fruit, and peppermint patties, Grandmomma's favorite snack. After popping two chocolate stars into her mouth— and one of everything else into her pocket—Isabelle crossed her fingers. There was only one drawer left.

It was marked DO NOT OPEN. This had to be it!

Isabelle pulled on the handle. It was stuck. She braced one foot on the desk and pulled until—Eureka!

It popped open.

She held her breath. There was only one thing in the drawer: *The Official Rule Book for Fairy Godmothers, 11th Edition, Teacher's Guide.* Complete with Rules and Protocols, Quizzes, Appendix, and Frequently Asked Questions.

This was what gusto must feel like!

Isabelle opened the book and stared at the pages and pages of words and numbers and symbols. She brushed some loose sparkles off the first page and imagined what Clotilda would do if she walked into the room. She'd probably run straight to Grandmomma. Or cite some section of the rule book Isabelle had never heard of. No doubt, there'd even be a multiple-choice component.

"Opening up Grandmomma's rule book is a) totally cheating, b) very shortsighted, c) a mistake that could come back to haunt you, or d) all of the above."

Isabelle cracked herself up. Really, reading this book might technically be cheating, but when she thought about it, it wasn't that different from asking Clotilda or Grandmomma for some extra help. They'd been begging her to do that!

As the large grandfather clock in the corner began to chime, Isabelle opened the book to a page marked with a bright pink ribbon. More loose sparkles flickered onto the words. They were all the colors of nature—red, blue, yellow, and white—the colors that gave fairy godmothers their magic.

The first and most important secret to finding happily ever after is . . .

Isabelle held her breath and turned the page to look for the choices. She was sure this one thing was all she really needed to know!

And then she turned another page.

And another.

And another.

Instead of seeing words, she saw twinkles; she saw dust. Page after page, every single letter of every single word of every single rule was shimmering and disappearing before she had a chance to read them.

Sparkles! They really were powerful! And not always in a good way! Isabelle knew she had to get out of there before she caused any more damage.

Isabelle shoved the book back in the drawer and headed for the door, but then she stopped and stared at all the piles of sparkles.

Before she could consider the consequences, Isabelle grabbed two giant handfuls of gold sparkles and stuffed them in her pockets. Grandmomma wouldn't miss them. She had plenty. And they just might come in handy.

Isabelle hurried down the halls, up the stairs, and around the corners of the castle as fast as she could. She held in the urge to pump her fists and sing fairy godmother power anthems—that would be a giveaway. Most of all, she didn't want to run into Clotilda—or even worse, Grandmomma. She didn't need a rule book to tell her that two pocketfuls of borrowed sparkles was grounds for immediate banishment.

Safe in her room, Isabelle emptied her pockets into a spare jar with a tight lid. She hid the jar in the one and only place Clotilda never dared to snoop: her underwear drawer.

She tried to nap, but her head spun from too many sparkles, and her stomach hurt, too—but that was probably guilt.

Guilt did not make last-minute studying easier. It didn't make her happier, either, especially when Clotilda knocked on her door with tea and toast with a sprinkling of cinnamon sugar. "It's normal to be nervous," Clotilda said. "But you're *my* sister. You can't be anything but great."

Isabelle and Clotilda might be sisters, but Isabelle didn't think they had anything else in common. Isabelle looked and acted more like another infamous fairy godmother—their mom.

And, as Grandmomma liked to remind her, that was not a favorable comparison.

Chapter Three

Ready or Not

The next morning, as Isabelle made her way out the door to the Official Fairy Godmother Training Center, her stomach still felt like it was twisting in knots. Or maybe *knots* wasn't the right word. Really, her whole body felt more like it was full of pointy magic wands—and not in a good way at all.

When she reached the entrance of the training center, Isabelle almost turned around. To enter the room, she had to choose between two doors. This was so discouraging.

She couldn't believe she had to take a test before she'd ever set foot in a classroom!

The door on the right was covered in glitter and bright colors. The words WALK THROUGH THIS DOOR IF YOU ARE READY TO BECOME A GREAT FAIRY GODMOTHER flashed brightly across it. The door on the left was not fancy at all. It was brown and smooth, and it felt a lot like leather. The words on this door were small and looked a little bit blurry, so she stepped right up to them. WALK THROUGH THIS DOOR IF YOU ARE NOT.

Why did there always have to be multiple choices?

Why did she always feel like she was about to be tricked?

Claiming to be ready seemed like the smart thing to say, but it was also less humble. Humility, according to Clotilda, was the fifth most important thing a fairy godmother had to be.

When a really old godmother showed up, Isabelle did not waste a second. "Which door is the right one?" she asked.

The old godmother looked her up and down. "They're both the same," she said, limping past her toward the brown door. "Everyone is ready. And everyone is not."

That sounded suspiciously like something Clotilda would make up. But since Isabelle wanted to get a look around the classroom before Grandmomma arrived, she didn't question the old godmother. Instead, she squared her shoulders and confidently walked through the fancy door. She decided to look ready, even though she wasn't.

The truth was nobody inside even looked up to see which door she had picked. They were too busy talking and looking around the room. Photographs of the greatest fairy godmothers of all time—including a nice picture of Grandmomma as a young godmother—covered the back wall. Above the photos flashed everyone's favorite slogan: HAPPILY EVER AFTER. THE LAST LINE OF EVERY GREAT STORY.

The front of the room was interesting, too. There was a big red desk and an even bigger red chair. On the desk sat a jar full of pencils and a bigger jar full of candy. It was stocked with all of Grandmomma's favorites, and some of Isabelle's, too. She recognized the wrappers from her secret trip to Grandmomma's office.

Next, Isabelle looked for an empty seat.

Normally when there was listening to do, she preferred to sit in the back row. But three older godmothers, including the really old one she had met outside, had already taken those spots. Isabelle figured they were probably teachers, since they looked just like Grandmomma on a bad day: crabby, tired, and annoyed.

The only two other people in the room were young like her. But they had taken seats in the one place she did not want to sit—the front row, right in front of Grandmomma's desk.

The first girl reminded her of an intricate flower. Her black hair was piled into fancy braids with red and pink ribbons and scarves that made her dark skin glow. Her arms looked strong and lean, like the roots and stems of the flowers that grew all over the eastern half of the fairy godmother world.

The second one looked like she had drifted down from the clouds in the sky. Like a lot of fairy godmothers of the past, she was more bubble than brawn, all pinks and whites and pale yellows and fluff. She had very round eyes and very round cheeks and a very round body.

Isabelle thought about sitting down next to them, but they looked so cool and confident that she couldn't help but feel a little intimidated.

Clotilda had told Isabelle (about a million times) that, just like princesses, fairy godmothers came in all shapes, sizes, and shades. She'd also told her that as she progressed in the training, she would learn about all the different customs of princesses as well as the godmothers. And that she was going to make great lifelong friends.

But these girls—she didn't know what to say. They looked polished and smart and so much more . . . well, everything. Plus, they were reading *The Official Rule Book for Fairy*

Godmothers like it was the most interesting book they'd ever seen. No matter how many times Isabelle coughed or cleared her throat or yawned really loudly, they didn't look up. Hopefully that meant they weren't prepared, either.

She was still standing when the really old fairy godmother from earlier waved her over.

"What are you waiting for—an invitation?" the old godmother whispered. "Go on, introduce yourself. They won't bite!"

Isabelle knew better than to disappoint a teacher! As fast as she could, she walked back up the aisle and stood in front of the two girls. "Hello there. My name is Isabelle. I am very much pleased to meet you." Her voice came out sounding more like a frog croak than real words. Neither girl looked up.

Isabelle tried again, this time speaking louder and slower. "Hello," she said. "I'm Isabelle."

This time, they perked up. "As in, sister of *the* Clotilda?"

Isabelle nodded and both girls squealed. "The fourth best fairy godmother in the land," the girl with the braids said. "You must be so proud."

Isabelle didn't know about fourth best, but there was no point in arguing. "Yes. We're all really proud."

They asked her tons of questions, from Clotilda's favorite color (yellow) to what Clotilda liked to eat (peaches) and what she thought about Clotilda's princess, Melody (perfection, obviously). Neither one of them invited Isabelle to pull up a chair. But maybe they were nervous, too. Isabelle was willing to give them the benefit of the doubt. She sat down in the row behind them and waited for the Clotilda excitement to die down.

It took a while, but eventually the girl with the braids offered her name. "My name is Angelica. And this is Fawn."

When Fawn held out her hand, she looked like she might be in danger of floating away. "I'm so excited to get started. Aren't you?" She opened up her Wish List, the master portfolio of all the princesses past, present, and future, then looked at Isabelle's empty lap. "Where are your books? Don't tell me you're such a genius like your sister that you don't need them?"

Isabelle hadn't even thought about bringing her books. She'd never bothered to open the big, fat Wish List that came with the rule book. It was still in its wrapping, stacked in the corner of her room, collecting dust.

But Isabelle knew better than to admit all that. Instead she winked—the way you do when you have a secret—with her mouth wide open (and perhaps a stray sparkle near her eye). She said, "I'd rather not talk about princesses, if you know what I mean."

To her surprise, Angelica seemed to know exactly what she meant. She pointed to the old godmothers in the back of the room. "We don't want to say anything in front of the Worsts, either." She rolled her eyes and whispered, "I couldn't believe it when I saw them!"

"They're the Worsts? Really?" Isabelle said, too

surprised to whisper. She had heard that Grandmomma liked to readmit the most unsuccessful fairy godmothers for retraining—to give them a fresh start—but she hadn't expected them to look so normal. "I thought they were our teachers."

The really old godmother hit Isabelle in the head with a crumpled-up piece of paper. "You know, we can hear you." On the paper was a drawing of Grandmomma. It was not complimentary.

The Worsts all began complaining at once:

"The system is rigged."

"She acts like she's doing us a favor."

"Some princesses like being miserable. Don't say we didn't warn you. It was a lot better. Before."

Isabelle knew what she meant by "before." She meant before Mom and her really unhappy princess, before all the new rules, when fairy godmothers didn't have to go to training—or in their case, retraining. "What do you mean, 'rigged'?"

The really old one had tons of wrinkles. "You'll see soon enough."

One of her friends had bright purple hair and a very long nose. "How do you think your sister got to be fourth best? In the old days, you had to pay your dues!"

Isabelle still didn't know about fourth best, but she didn't want to argue. "Clearly, you haven't met Clotilda." Her sister had always been perfect and talented and got everything she wanted way before anyone else. "Besides, Grandmomma would never rig the system. She's not that nice." She smiled. "The truth is, most of the time she's crabby. And stuffy. And . . ."

"Isabelle."

Angelica and Fawn went back to reading. The Worsts looked away.

A shadow crept across the room.

Isabelle felt a cold, bony hand on her shoulder. She did not have to turn around to see whom it belonged to.

Chapter Four

The Long and Difficult First Day.
Part One

In case it wasn't clear, a cold bony hand on the shoulder is never a good sign. Especially when it belongs to Grandmomma.

"Welcome to Level One," she said, walking to the front of the class. "I hope you're all excited to be here."

Angelica and Fawn stood up and clapped their hands. They were definitely excited.

The Worsts didn't budge or smile. They definitely were not.

Grandmomma spelled out the rules for training. "First you will have to succeed in the classroom. Only then will you get a chance to demonstrate what you've learned on one practice princess chosen especially for you."

Isabelle was pleased that she knew all of this already. "And if you make her happy, you get to go to the Extravaganza! Am I right?" Isabelle asked. She popped up out of her seat, eager to show Grandmomma she had done *some* studying.

"Not just happy, Isabelle. *Happily ever after.*" Grandmomma's whole face turned as red as a rose. "Now, please sit down. You should be more focused on graduating to Level Two than going to a party. I don't want to talk about the Extravaganza right now."

Isabelle sank down in her seat, slightly deflated.

The Extravaganza wasn't just any party. According to Clotilda, it was the best, most magical can't-miss party of every fairy godmother season. On that night, godmothers near and far dressed up in fancy clothes and ate delicious food. They took turns showing off their amazing magical skills. Clotilda had told Isabelle that last year, one fairy godmother made an entire garden of flowers bloom. Another brightened the sky with brand-new stars. And that was not all. Officially, the Extravaganza was also a meeting where fairy godmothers traded and picked up new princesses. But Isabelle wasn't certain how that part worked.

As Grandmomma continued to talk, Isabelle thought of another question. This time, she raised her hand and waited for Grandmomma to call on her.

Grandmomma nodded at Isabelle. "Yes?"

"When do we get our wands?" Isabelle asked.

Grandmomma sighed and went right back to addressing the class. She talked about the early history of fairy god-mothers, the times when they only served royal princesses, because they were the only ones who believed in magic. Then she talked about a time after that when *everyone* believed in magic and fairy godmothers were busy 24-7.

Then she skipped over a whole lot of bad things (even though they all knew what she was talking about) and reviewed some of the things they were going to learn and do during the different levels of training and how it was important to do something or other. To be honest, Isabelle sort of lost track when it became clear that Grandmomma was not going to talk about wands.

During the lecture, Isabelle drew bunny ears on the Worsts' drawing of Grandmomma. Then she added a cute bow tie. Then she turned the paper over and drew 227 squares that were all the same size. She would have colored them in, but Grandmomma flicked her wand at Isabelle, turning the paper into a teeny tiny orange, otherwise known as a kumquat.

Just thinking about the word *kumquat* made Isabelle want to laugh. Since she knew this would be a bad thing to do, she pinched her nose to hold it in. As it turned out, this was a bad strategy. All it did was make her laugh come out like a snort, and as anyone who has ever laughed at the wrong moment knows, snorts were even funnier than *kumquat*, and *kumquat* was an objectively funny word.

"Isabelle!" Grandmomma flicked her wand again to make the kumquat disappear in a cloud of orange sparkles. "Did you hear what I just said about the official fairy godmother practice princess system?"

Isabelle coughed, stalling for time. "Um . . . I believe you said that there was no such thing as a lousy princess?" This was a guess, but it was a good one. She said that all the time.

Grandmomma picked up her teacher's guide and began to read:

"The difference between a practice princess and the princess you receive when you are a real fairy godmother is a) Not much. All of them want to be happy, b) Everything. Fairy godmothers in training have one cycle (also known as a season) to make their practice princesses happy. Real fairy godmothers serve their princesses for a much longer time, c) Age. Fairy godmothers in training are paired with princesses who are young, whose wishes are small and easy to grant." She made quotation marks with her fingers when she said the word *wishes*.

Isabelle waited for her to say *d*, but instead Grand-momma tapped her wand on her desk. "But when I say 'wishes,' there are conditions, as I'm sure you're all aware." (That's what the air quotes were for.) She continued, "But if not, please see the appendix, sections 3.5, 3.6, and 3.7, at your earliest possible convenience. Clear?"

Isabelle said "Clear" along with the rest of the class, even though she had definitely not read the appendix (or anything else in the rule book, really).

Again, Grandmomma tapped her wand on the desk. This time, a few sparks flew out of the tip. "So, who can tell me what the answer is?"

Angelica's hand shot up like a sunflower. "All of the above, of course." It was clear that she already knew every word of the manual. "The system works perfectly because we get the right princess at the right time."

Fawn added in a wispy voice, "We are so grateful for this opportunity. We know you will set us up to do great things." She opened the book to a page in the middle. "I especially like your tips for looking like a pro."

Grandmomma was clearly not above flattery. "Thank you both," she said, pointing her wand at the candy jar. Two pieces popped out of the jar and whisked up and around the room before landing on Angelica's and Fawn's desks.

Isabelle raised her hand before she knew what she wanted to say. The sound of candy wrappers crinkling made her mouth water. "Can I—"

"Silence!" Grandmomma shook her head, but she didn't look that annoyed. "Without further ado," she said, "I have something far better for all of you."

Right on cue, trumpets began to blare. Drums pounded. Something huge was about to happen.

Because of the music, Grandmomma had to shout to be heard. "Happily ever after requires more than magic. It is about so much more than sparkles." She laughed. "But neither one of those things hurts, either!"

When the music ended, she pointed to the back door and everyone turned around. She said, "To celebrate your first day of training, please welcome my dearest friends, the worldwide experts on happily ever after."

Standing at the door were the top three ranking fairy godmothers in the world, the best of the best. No introduction was necessary.

Chapter Five

The Long and Difficult First Day, Part Two

Isabelle had seen the Bests plenty of times—but only from a safe distance.

Up close was different. Up close, they all looked so powerful and proud—and even a little bit scary. They seemed totally different from the other godmothers she'd met. As they walked to the front of the room, they held their wands high in the air, almost as high as their noses.

This made them look a little stuck up, but Isabelle figured it was most likely a safety precaution. Since they were all literally on the job, their wands had to be loaded with tons of sparkles. Thanks to Clotilda, Isabelle knew that Number Two thought she should be Number One, and Number Three had a lot of new ideas. One false move and anything might happen.

Number One introduced herself first.

"Good morning, trainees! My name is Luciana, but my first princess called me Luciana the *Fascinante*, and let's just say the name stuck."

Unlike Clotilda and Grandmomma, Luciana wore her dark brown bun at the base of her neck. A jeweled ribbon and a carnation finished the look. Very sophisticated.

She flicked her wrist, and a bundle of pure white carnations appeared on every single desk. "That princess, Nina Valentina, wasn't just beautiful—she was also spoiled rotten. And what a temper! She threw tantrum after tantrum until the king himself was afraid to cross her on even the smallest of requests." She tapped her wand again, and the carnations turned red—just like the one in her hair. "That's when I was called in."

The story of Nina and Luciana was one of the first ones Isabelle had ever heard. The way Grandmomma told it, Nina was the kind of princess that they all wished for. She was intelligent and feisty, a born leader, and a rascal.

"Making Nina happily ever after wasn't easy," Luciana said, "but when I was done, she knew how to appreciate her good fortune. She became a wise ruler. She is still remembered for her humility and kindness to all living things."

When everyone was done cheering, Number Two stepped forward. She wore a colorful floor-length smock, cinched tightly at the waist. Her voice was soft and deep, and she spoke very slowly. "My name is Raine."

Isabelle thought that was a perfect name for her. She was tall and dark-skinned with bright yellow hair. "Were you named for the weather?"

Angelica turned around and glared at her. "What is wrong with you? Her name means Queen."

As Isabelle slumped in her chair, Raine whipped out her wand and held it high over her head. Poof! Crack! Bam! Grandmomma's dress turned into a beautiful orange, black, and green robe—not that different from Raine's. "As you should know from your Wish List, I received my first princess right after she'd been kidnapped by a witch, so I had to think fast. I turned myself into a starling and taught her how to understand me, so she would never feel alone. I also made the most beautiful tree you can imagine."

"That was such a great idea," Angelica said.

Isabelle was confused. Why a tree? Why a bird? In this case, being a fairy godmother seemed even more complicated than she had imagined.

Raine smiled in a nostalgic way. "Legend says that as my princess grew older, people told the king of that beautiful tree, and that because he had to see it, he found the princess. And that's fine for them to believe, but you should know I did everything. I sang in the king's ear and told him to look for the tree. Although I'm not as famous or sensational as some other fairy godmothers, I don't mind. Legends are all part of the job." She gave Luciana the side eye. "Remember: We are helpers. It's not about us. Princesses need to learn to be independent. They can't just wait around for happily ever after."

Angelica looked like she was about to say something, but then the lights went out, and an empty spotlight appeared at the front of the room. Then it moved to the back of the room. When it moved back to the front, Number Three was ready. She held her arms out wide. "My name is Kaminari." As she walked around the room, her hair swooshed and shined like she'd powdered it with sparkles—like it was made of black glass.

"Trainees, my first princess was a beggar girl named Jade. Right after I met her, she was tossed into a river by a greedy young man who couldn't see her royal heart."

"So you swooped down and saved her from the river?" Isabelle asked.

"No. I let a nice couple do that." Kaminari winked. "FYI, fairy godmothers do not save princesses." She picked up her wand and twirled it through her fingers. "Once she was safe, I helped her understand forgiveness— to see the good in all people, even the greedy young man. Of course, I also gave her a ton of jewels. What's a princess without jewels?" When she was done reminiscing, she blew on the end of her wand, spraying everyone in the room with piles of red and gold sparkles.

Before Isabelle could try stuffing them in her pockets, Kaminari opened her arms. "Being a fairy godmother can be fun. But it is also serious business. If you stick around long enough, you can change the world." Without saying another word, all the sparkles disappeared.

After each Best took a bow and exited the classroom, Grandmomma returned to the front of the room. She told them all to quiet down. (In other words, the fun part was over.) "Trainees, the art of wand waving is the most essential skill a fairy godmother can master. Your style is important. But it is the substance and heart you bring to your style that matter most."

Fawn wrote something down in her book. She tried to cover her writing, but Isabelle could still see it. *When you help your princess, good things happen.*

"Is that always true?" Isabelle said out loud by accident.

Grandmomma placed a piece of candy on her desk. "I suggest that every chance you can, you get to work. As you just heard, sometimes you have to act fast. Sometimes, your work will seem unconventional. Prepare to get to know your princess, so you are ready for her wish. Know her strengths and weaknesses as well as the part of the world she lives in. Most important, always ask: How can I help?"

"Does that mean we're going to get our wands now?" Isabelle asked. She stopped herself from adding *finally*.

But Grandmomma could tell that's what she was thinking. "First you need to earn them, Isabelle. Also, you need to do some paperwork."

A huge stack of documents appeared on each desk in a small cloud of sparkles. The first page said:

Official Fairy Godmother Contract. Please read carefully.

Angelica and Fawn seemed charmed, but the Worsts grumbled. "How exciting," they said. "Just what we were hoping for."

Grandmomma acted like she hadn't heard a single moan or groan. "When you've read everything, please sign your name on the line and clip all the pages together. In exchange," she said, "I will give you what you've all been waiting for." She glanced at Isabelle but did not crack a smile. "Remember, take your time. Read every single word. Do not skip the fine print."

Isabelle looked down at the very thick stack of papers.

I, _____, do solemnly swear to uphold all the rules and guidelines in *The Official Rule Book for Fairy Godmothers, 11th Edition.*

In her opinion, all the print was fine. The letters all ran together. If she stared at it too long, they turned blurry and wavy. Isabelle found it impossible to sit still long enough to even read the second line.

Really, what did it matter? She knew what would happen if she succeeded. She knew what would happen if she failed.

If the fine print was so important, Grandmomma should have made it bigger.

Isabelle pretended to read. She turned one page, then another and another, over and over again.

When she got to the very last page, she whipped out a pen with a dramatic flick of her wrist and signed her name on the line. Then she ran to the big red desk and plopped all those papers into Grandmomma's arms.

"I'm done first," she said. "Aren't you impressed? Can I have my wand now?"

"Practice wand," Grandmomma reminded Isabelle, reaching into a desk drawer and pulling out a small, plain stick. "Once you pass training, then we will give it some juice."

Isabelle tried to hide her disappointment as she accepted the non-magical stick.

"What do you say?" Grandmomma prompted her.

Isabelle grinned. "Wait until you see my signature style. You are going to love it."

The really old godmother cleared her throat. Loudly. Then she coughed twice.

Isabelle knew what that meant. "I mean, thank you. And I am ready and humble and excited. I promise. I understand the terms of the contract."

Grandmomma shooed her out the door. "So you say," she said. "So you say."

Chapter Six

Girlgoyles Make Excellent (Practice) Princesses

The next day, Isabelle tried her best to do everything she was told.

She ran around cones—for agility. She did ballet—for grace. She even played the trust game. In her opinion, this game was so boring it shouldn't even be called a game, but for some reason, it was really important to Grandmomma. To play the trust game, each fairy godmother had to pick a partner. Then (without looking) each of them had to take a turn falling into her partner's arms.

Isabelle was chosen last.

"Stand closer," the really old godmother said. Her name was Minerva. "And put down your wand."

"I can do two things at once." Isabelle had tied a ribbon to the end of her practice wand to make it look fancier. When she flicked her wrist, the ribbon zigged and zagged. It made her look almost magical.

Minerva snatched it out of her hands. She was a lot stronger than she looked. "If you drop me, I'll turn you into a grasshopper. Don't think I can't."

Isabelle wondered if it would be fun to be a grasshopper, if only for a minute. She also wondered if she should bring in her own sparkles (the stolen ones in her underwear drawer).

Luckily, everyone else was paying attention. "Watch out!" they shouted at Isabelle. "Don't drop her!"

Isabelle dove for the ground just in time for Minerva to land in her lap. "Told you I wouldn't drop you," she said.

Then she turned to Grandmomma. "Now do we get some sparkles?"

Grandmomma called them all to her desk. "How about one?" According to her, this was plenty of magic. Grandmomma turned to the Bests, who were joining them for their first lesson with sparkles. "They're all yours," she said grimly.

Luciana the *Fascinante* called them to the front of the room. "Let's start with the basics of incorporating sparkles into your magic." She dropped a pile of rags on the floor. "To start, I'd like you to transform this mess into appropriate princess attire." She made it sound like it was the easiest thing in the world to do.

Tap, tap, tap! Angelica made a blue dress on her third try. Tap, tap, tap! Fawn managed to make a cool pair of gold pants. Isabelle hunched her shoulders. The Worsts went ahead of her. They all made gowns. (They were very old-fashioned.)

Luciana pointed her wand straight at Isabelle's heart. "Why don't you give it a try now?"

Tap, tap, tap! Isabelle pointed her wand at the pile of cloth. Tap, tap, tap! They flopped around a bit. Tap, tap, tap, tap, tap, tap, TAP! The rags whirled up in the air and got tangled around a statue of the greatest fairy god-mother ever (may she rest in peace), knocked over the jar full of candy, and almost tripped up Minerva (but luckily she got out of the way in time).

"Too many taps!" Luciana no longer looked *fascinante*, unless *fascinante* meant furious.

"Let's go outside," Raine said. She handed each of them a live mouse as they exited the classroom. "We can clean this up later."

"Cheer up! No sulking allowed," Minerva told Isabelle as they claimed their mice and followed the others. "Not everyone is a dressmaker. Maybe you'll do better with livestock."

This turned out to be wishful thinking.

When they got outside, Angelica volunteered to go first (of course). She managed to turn her mouse into a brown-and-white pony on the second try. Fawn was even better. Her mouse became a unicorn.

Isabelle was too busy enjoying the fresh air to keep good track of her mouse.

When Raine asked her to take a turn, Isabelle tried to fake it. (She couldn't admit she had no idea where her mouse was hiding.) She aimed her wand at a nearby shadow.

Pop! A kangaroo appeared! And it didn't look happy.

This was a disaster!

Everyone knew that fairy godmothers were supposed to respect the animal kingdom. They were not supposed to lose their mice or turn just anything into a creature that was supposed to stay wild. "What were you thinking?" Minerva asked. Raine looked furious. Grandmomma was already apologizing.

Isabelle shook her wand. "I think it's defective. Or maybe I need more sparkles."

It was frustrating to have magic that didn't work—maybe even more frustrating than having no magic at all.

"You do not need any more sparkles." Minerva whipped out her wand and pointed it at Isabelle's unhappy kangaroo. "Use a little more body in your flick. Think before you wave." In one motion, the kangaroo turned into a happy, sleepy puppy.

Isabelle wanted to hug her. Like everyone else, she'd felt bad for the kangaroo. "You are so not a Worst fairy godmother," she whispered.

Minerva picked up the puppy and scratched it behind its ears. "Tonight, practice with something simple. Like a piece of fruit." She added, "If it's a little soft, it's easier to transform."

After class, Isabelle hurried home to the girlgoyles.

"Would you like a dress? Or maybe some new shoes? Or how about a gigantic purple helicopter to fly you all over the world until we find Mom?" (If Isabelle could grant her own wish, that's what she would want.)

The girlgoyles, of course, made excellent practice princesses. They were patient. They didn't argue. They didn't complain when the ripe peach did not turn into anything special. Isabelle could tell they loved the way the ribbon swirled in the air when she flicked her wrist. If they could talk, she was sure they would tell her how magical she looked when she held her wand high above her head toward the stars.

But they couldn't talk, so Isabelle kept practicing. It was fun to pretend that she was good at this.

First she added a full-body twirl to her wand routine, but it was hard to stop at just one. So she tried three. Then five. Five was fun, but it made her so dizzy she tipped over. After she had fallen so many times that both knees required first aid, she settled on a twirl and a half followed by a fancy over-and-under jabbing action.

Then Isabelle went downstairs to her sister's room so she could demonstrate her new moves for an expert. "What do you think? Incredible, right?"

"Incredibly wrong. Are you taking advice from Minerva?"

Clotilda preferred a simple (boring) flick of the wrist followed by a teeny tiny (also boring) figure-eight motion. "You don't want to freak anyone out. Practice princesses aren't ready for a full-strength fairy godmother. Why do you think Minerva was sent back into training?"

Isabelle stamped her foot. Then she paced around the room. There were too many rules. In her opinion, twirls made her very trustworthy. And a lot more interesting.

Clotilda apologized in a kind-but-annoying way. "If it helps, everyone's nervous in the beginning."

"Not you. Not Grandmomma."

"Especially me. Especially Grandmomma."

Isabelle couldn't imagine Grandmomma being nervous about anything. "But what if I can't do it? What if I'm never good enough? What if I get a princess . . . like *her*?"

When she said "her," she meant the unhappy princess who had changed everything. Clotilda put her hand over Isabelle's mouth. "Grandmomma wouldn't do that."

Isabelle shut Clotilda's bedroom door. She did not want Grandmomma walking in on them. "What's the use? I'm just like her."

This time by "her," she meant Mom.

Clotilda sat down next to Isabelle. She pulled back her sister's unruly hair. "Just because you look like her and act like her doesn't mean you'll mess up like her." She tried to sound encouraging. "Don't forget, you have a rule book. You get to go to training. She didn't have any of that."

That did not make Isabelle feel any better. "You don't understand. You're perfect. You always have been. And I'm . . ."

"Learning. That's all," Clotilda said in a perky way. "How about I quiz you? Or I can show you some more wand tips."

But Isabelle didn't want any tips.

"Maybe if you tell me the story," Isabelle said, "I'll feel better."

So, even though this was a story Clotilda didn't enjoy telling, she agreed to tell it just this once. The truth was Clotilda missed their mother, too. Most importantly, no matter how snooty and perfect she might seem, she really wanted her sister to do well.

Chapter Seven

The Story of the Worst Fairy Godmother, According to Clotilda

Warning: This is a sad story.

Once upon a time, a long time ago, back when there weren't many princesses or fairy godmothers and there wasn't even a rule book, there lived a very young and very lively fairy godmother. She was known for her pure heart and beautiful laugh. Every day, she could be found dancing around the fairy godmother world.

She was very talented, so she was paired with the most beautiful and beloved princess the regular world had ever known.

This princess was sweet and smart and kind to everyone she met. Every time she made a wish, her fairy godmother took out her wand and her sparkles and got to work. It was so much fun making her princess happily ever after. So she got some more sparkles. And then just a few more.

The fairy godmother didn't listen to warnings that sparkles should be used in moderation. She didn't realize that if she used too many sparkles, they could stop working altogether.

One day, the fairy godmother's magic was—poof!— gone. She couldn't make any more wishes come true. Her princess was distraught. She cried over everything— even puppies. Or kittens. Or something like a glass of spilled milk. Her fairy godmother tried everything to get her magic back. She would not give up.

One day, the princess became so unhappy that she decided she didn't want to be a princess anymore. She gave up her crown and ran away. She told her fairy godmother to leave her alone—forever.

People all over the land cried for their lost princess. But they never blamed her. They didn't blame the king or the queen (who usually got blamed for these things).

Instead, they blamed her fairy godmother. And because they blamed her, all girls stopped making wishes. They stopped believing in magic. And that meant the fairy godmothers had no one to make happy. For a very long time, they didn't have anything to do.

This was a very dark and lonely time.

A world without fairy godmothers, without wishing, without happily ever afters, was too grim. The elder godmothers decided they had to do something.

So they came up with new rules. They started training new godmothers. They guaranteed the regular world that every single princess would get a wise and careful and smart fairy godmother—one who knew all the rules and didn't take too many risks.

And the fairy godmother who lost her magic?

The fairy godmothers took away her wand and her sparkles. Even though they didn't want to, they told her she could no longer be a fairy godmother. This is another sad part: Even though she promised to be good and quiet and not make any more trouble, they told her she could no longer live in the fairy godmother world.

In the name of happily ever after, she had to leave.

So she did.

And this is the really sad part: She was never heard from again.

Chapter Eight

There's No Such Thing as a Lousy Princess

When testing day arrived, Grandmomma stood at the front of the room in a long dress and presidential cape. "The time has come," she said, raising her wand, "to see if you are ready to receive your practice princesses."

Angelica went first. She touched her hip with the tip of her wand, and then raised her arm high over her head. It was very dramatic. It also made her look even more like a flower than usual.

Grandmomma looked impressed. "Tell me. When is the right time to greet your princess for the first time?"

Isabelle froze. She didn't remember Grandmomma telling them they had to answer questions on the spot.

Angelica didn't seem fazed at all. "After they have wished for something that will make them happy." Then she added, "But it is also prudent not to visit her immediately or too often. In fact, in many cases, it is better to help your princess without being seen or heard. A good fairy godmother knows what to do." She started to list a few examples, but Grandmomma held up her hand and told her to return to her seat.

It was Fawn's turn next. "Step forward," Grandmomma said. Fawn stood up, held out her arms, and appeared to float across the room. In front of Grandmomma, she swirled her wand in the air like she was stirring up a cloud.

Isabelle was totally impressed. Her style was really cool. Better than Angelica's, even.

Grandmomma appeared to agree. "Are all princesses real princesses?" she asked with a smile.

"They used to be." Fawn held up a finger and said, "But now there are exceptions. It is possible to draw a girl who wants to become a princess. Or someone with princess-like wishes."

(Isabelle wasn't sure what a princess-like wish was. But she couldn't ask. Not during testing.)

"Are there any other exceptions?" Grandmomma asked.

Fawn did not answer right away. "Technically, it's possible for fairy godmothers to help regular girls—but I don't know of any recent examples."

This answer made Isabelle squirm. Regular did not sound like a good thing to be. Regular sounded bad, like *normal* in the Fairy Godmother Home for Normal Girls.

As the Worsts took their turns, Isabelle could think about nothing but normal and regular. Regular and normal.

When Grandmomma called her name, she was still worried.

Isabelle walked to the front of the room, held up her wand, and tried to look Grandmomma in the eye. This was not easy. She blinked twice, and then a third and fourth time. But Grandmomma didn't blink at all. That made Isabelle blink even more.

"Your signature style?" Grandmomma prompted.

Isabelle tried to be brave, but right away, her performance went wrong. First, she forgot to curtsy. Then her half twirl turned into a quarter turn and an almost trip. Third, her swoosh looked more like a swish.

Grandmomma didn't smile, but she didn't frown, either. "I have a special question for you. What is the first and most important secret to finding happily ever after?"

That question sounded familiar to Isabelle, like she had seen it somewhere before . . .

Then she realized it was the question from the rule book—the one whose answer had disappeared when she snuck into Grandmomma's office.

Isabelle was pretty sure this was not a coincidence.

"There is no secret," Isabelle said finally. She waited for Grandmomma to tell her to pack her bags and go to a brand-new terrible place called the Home for Incompetent Fairy Godmothers Who Could Never Be Trusted.

Instead, Grandmomma thanked her. She said, "I'll be back soon." As she walked out the door, Clotilda walked in. She told the group she was here to keep them busy while Grandmomma discussed them with the three Bests.

For the first time ever, Isabelle didn't mind waiting.

Minerva didn't, either. "I told you the whole thing is rigged," she said. "But maybe for you, that's not a bad thing."

"What is that supposed to mean?" Isabelle asked.

Minerva looked a little embarrassed. "Well, she is your grandmother."

When Grandmomma and the Bests came back, Isabelle crossed all her fingers and toes. She wasn't sure if her performance had been enough to get her assigned a practice princess.

Bright lights suddenly filled the classroom. Confetti fell from the ceiling. (Isabelle was pretty sure this was the work of Kaminari.)

"Congratulations to all of you," Grandmomma said. "You have all passed."

"That's amazing!" Isabelle jumped out of her seat and danced around the room. She tried to hug Angelica, but Angelica did not want to be hugged. Neither did Fawn.

When she tried to hug Minerva, the old godmother accepted a short embrace. "We can celebrate later." (She looked happy, too.) "Right now we have to pay attention. Your grandmother wants to say something."

Isabelle sat down and watched Grandmomma uncover a huge bowl filled with sparkles. "I will call you forward, best to worst. You will receive information about your practice princess. Then you will dip your wand in the sparkles. These sparkles will give you just enough magic to help your practice princesses."

Isabelle almost clapped her hands when Grandmomma pulled out the first envelope.

"Congratulations, Fawn," Grandmomma said. "You may begin."

Isabelle could hardly believe it when Fawn dipped her wand into the bowl. She thought she might have heard a sizzling sound. When Fawn removed her wand, the top half had turned white. She looked different, too. A little older. And happier.

When Fawn opened her envelope, she discovered that her practice princess had already made a wish. She wanted to see snow.

Isabelle was not impressed. "Snow? Are you kidding?" That didn't seem like a hard wish to make come true.

No surprise, Angelica earned the next-highest score. When she dipped her wand into the sparkles, it made a crackling sound. When she opened her envelope, it revealed a beautiful princess who wanted to sail a ship.

That didn't seem hard to make happen, either, but before Isabelle could say anything, Minerva hit Isabelle in the head with a balled-up piece of paper. When Isabelle looked back, Minerva gave her a look that clearly said "Be quiet."

Everyone was surprised when Grandmomma called Minerva next. She looked like she was about to cry when she opened her envelope and saw the great-great-great-granddaughter of her first and most beloved princess. (Minerva was *really* old.)

Next, Grandmomma called the other two Worsts, Irene and MaryEllen. Their styles had been simple. Their assignments didn't seem hard, either. In fact, everyone's practice princesses seemed like they were going to be really easy—nothing like the princesses and wishes the Bests had described.

That's what Isabelle was thinking about when Grand-momma called her to the front of the room.

It took her a second to realize that she was the final fairy godmother trainee to get a princess. The bottom of the barrel. The worst in the room.

Today, she didn't care. She was going to dip her wand into the sparkles. She was going to get a practice princess. Nothing else mattered.

"Thank you, Grandma," she said. "I know I can make my first princess happily ever after."

Grandmomma's eye twitched. She didn't like being called Grandma. "As you know," she told the class, the Bests, and Clotilda, who seemed to be crying, or at least dabbing her eye with her finger, "this is a big day for my family."

First, she pointed to the bowl. "Go ahead," she said. "Dip it in. Count to five. Feel the power of the sparkle."

Right away, Isabelle's wand began to turn white. Her hand shook. But it felt wonderful at the same time. She counted so slowly that when she got to three, Grandmomma yanked the bowl away. "That's all you need, Isabelle." She handed her the envelope. "Go on. Open it."

The room went silent. Everyone stared at the picture Isabelle held up.

"Sheesh. That's the worst princess I've ever seen," Minerva blurted out.

"She's actually not a princess," Grandmomma said. "Because of Isabelle's unique abilities, I have given her the first regular girl ever."

Isabelle shook out the envelope, but the picture was all there was. "Isn't there supposed to be a wish in here?" she asked Grandmomma.

Grandmomma didn't answer. Instead, she shooed Isabelle back to her seat. "Remember," she said to all of them, "you have one season and one season only to make your practice princess happily ever after. In the regular world, that means you've got a few weeks. Six weeks, to be exact, so please do not delay!"

As Isabelle walked out the door, Clotilda ran to her side and squeezed her hand in an annoying sisterly way. "Don't worry! All is not lost! You can watch me work first," she said. "Whoever this girl is, she can't be that bad."

Isabelle didn't agree. She might as well pack her bags now. It didn't matter how many sparkles she had hidden away.

Her princess was the girl whose picture she'd seen in the drawer in Grandmomma's office. She was the girl with the very sad frown and terrible hair and terrible everything.

Her name was Nora Silverstein.

Chapter Nine

Easy Peasy Lemon Squeezy

Three and a half days later, Clotilda sounded the alarm. "Isabelle! Come quick! It's happening."

Isabelle ran all the way down the hall. "Come quick" meant Melody was about to make a wish.

But when Isabelle got to Clotilda's room, nothing seemed out of place or even remotely magical. "Did I miss it?" Isabelle asked. "What's going on?" This was frustrating. "I don't hear or see or feel anything."

"You're not supposed to, but I can. Loud and clear."

Isabelle figured she had no choice but to sit down and trust her. "So what does she want?"

According to Clotilda, there was some big rodeo in town, and Melody had not yet been invited. Just like the princesses of classic fairy tales, she yearned to go and be part of the fun. She was a smart, nice, shy girl ready to saddle up on a horse and meet a smart, nice, shy boy. A prince, so to speak.

Melody even had a list of qualities she hoped he would possess. She wanted someone who

- liked board games,

- shared her love of going to the movies, and

- was kind to animals.

"No wonder Minerva thinks the system is rigged." It seemed to Isabelle that a rock with a stick taped to it could make this princess happy.

Clotilda disagreed. "Melody's wish might sound easy to you, but you have to understand: She isn't a practice princess. I'm going to be taking care of her for a long time." She took out her official Wish List and turned to the page that was all about Melody. "See how many things she wants? It's not like I jump every time she calls."

"So why this time?" Isabelle asked.

"Easy peasy lemon squeezy." Clotilda polished a spare apple, because she was very good at turning ripe fruit into fancy accessories. She also polished her wand and checked her hair (even though it was perfect). "Because she's sad. Because this one came from the heart." With that, Clotilda disappeared in a cloud of pink dust.

That was not an explanation.

Isabelle got up to leave. Behind the door, she found Grandmomma. She was snooping. "You want to watch?" she asked.

"Are you kidding?"

"I am not."

Grandmomma, who never kidded about anything, had a not-so-secret official fairy godmother spyglass to keep track of the godmothers, but in this case, she meant in person. "Forget the spyglass. Just hold on to me and whatever you do, don't let go while we're traveling."

A wave of the wand later, Isabelle sat in a corner of Melody's living room. She whispered, "Don't we need to hide?"

"Nope. And you don't have to whisper, either," Grandmomma said.

Isabelle, who had never been invisible before, danced around the room. She peered over Melody's shoulder as she read her party invitation. Isabelle wanted to try on Melody's cowboy hats, but Grandmomma put her foot down. "Calm down. You can look, but you can't touch."

When Melody started to pull dress after dress out of her closet, Isabelle decided to explore. She dragged

Grandmomma from room to room. Clothes were boring. Something smelled delicious.

Also, something didn't feel right. "Where's Clotilda? Isn't she supposed to be doing something?"

"What do you mean? She's doing everything." Grandmomma told Isabelle to sit down. She was getting tired. "Rule Seventeen: Foster independence. Please tell me you remember that."

"I remember," Isabelle said, even though she didn't. What was the fun in doing all the work but getting none of the credit?

It wasn't until Melody was almost ready to go that Clotilda appeared to add the finishing touches. She waved her wand and approved of all of Melody's choices. She also offered her good luck, confidence, and hope. She sprayed her with a few (non-magical) sparkles. These were just for show since she had already given Melody all of the things she needed.

"So what did you learn?" Grandmomma asked when they had returned to Isabelle's room.

Isabelle could feel a lecture coming. "I liked Melody's boots. They were snazzy and sensible."

"Your sister didn't get to be Number Four for nothing," Grandmomma said. "Now, open your rule book and think about everything you learned. Think about how Clotilda helped Melody. And for pity's sake, stay alert. There's magic in the air." She looked very excited—she was rarely wrong about these things. "This is it, Isabelle. Something tells me your Cinderella in the rough is going to make her wish soon."

Chapter Ten

Through the Spyglass:
A Longish Chapter Full of Problems

For what it's worth, calling Nora Silverstein a Cinderella in the rough was not really fair of Grandmomma.

According to Nora's very short entry in the Wish List, she did indeed have a stepmother, but that's where the similarities ended. Nora's stepmother was nice. Instead of a stepsister, Nora had a stepbrother, a cute little boy named Gregory, and he thought Nora was the greatest sister ever. Her father was a decent man. Mr. Silverstein rarely made her clean her very nice room that was not in the attic or under the stairs or some other unappealing place. Nora cared about serious things like school and nature and cooking and helping other people.

Isabelle didn't know what to do. There was no chapter in the rule book about serious princesses. There were no special rules for regular girls.

The next day, instead of taking Grandmomma's advice, Isabelle took a break. After all that training, she thought she deserved it. She ran laps around the castle until her feet and legs and arms were sore. She practiced some new moves with her wand. Six weeks was plenty of time to get down to business.

Clotilda thought this was foolish. "How do you expect to hear Nora make a wish if you don't sit still?"

So the next week, Isabelle sat. She sat in her room. She sat with the girlgoyles. She sat at the dinner table. She listened for Nora, but Nora didn't make a wish. Or maybe she made a wish, but Isabelle couldn't hear her.

Isabelle was sure she'd forgotten another rule (or that she hadn't learned it in the first place). She knocked on the heavy red door to Grandmomma's office.

For a change, Grandmomma didn't look crabby. "Tell me. Do you have news?" It turned out that Fawn had just created an off-season, once-in-a-lifetime snow shower for her princess. And Angelica's princess was already happily ever after, too, now that she had sailed across the Mediterranean Sea.

Isabelle felt like a failure. "It's not fair," she said. "You gave them easy princesses. Mine hasn't even made a wish yet."

Grandmomma popped a peppermint patty into her mouth. She repeated the same old things she always said: There is no such thing as a lousy princess. You get the right princess at the right time. Everyone deserves happily ever after. The magic didn't come from sparkles alone. Blah blah blah. "Are you trying to tell me you can't get it done?"

Isabelle didn't want to give up, but she didn't want to fail, either. Mostly, she didn't want to be like Mom. (But she didn't say any of those things.)

"Can we go snoop on her—the way we did with Melody? I promise to stand still. I won't touch a thing. Or if you're too tired, I could put on a disguise and follow her around."

Grandmomma sighed. She looked exhausted. It was hard to deny a girl willing to beg for someone else's happiness.

"Why don't you come back tomorrow and try the spyglass?" She made Isabelle promise not to tell anyone. "If Minerva gets wind of this, she'll have a conniption."

The next day, Isabelle returned to Grandmomma's office and peered through the spyglass. Grandmomma's magic spyglass could be used to transport fairy godmothers, or to simply observe princesses in their natural habitats.

Isabelle wanted to do the latter. She watched Nora eat breakfast. She watched her at school. She watched her say hello to two girls. She zoomed in.

Two girls meant friends.

It meant activities.

And maybe boys.

But instead of making plans, Nora told them she was taking her brother on a hike. She didn't make any plans. She let the girls walk away.

Isabelle hoped this was a good thing, since a lot of magic could happen in the woods. But in this case, it was another false alarm. Nora didn't run around or sing or talk to animals the way princesses were supposed to. Instead, she collected rocks. She spent a long time looking for lizards and caterpillars and feeding them leaves. Most of the time, she sat quietly in a clearing while her brother built a dirt castle. Later, they perched together on a log that someone had turned into a bench.

That night, Clotilda quizzed Isabelle about her Nora research. "Who are her friends? What does she like to do? Would she like a pet?"

A pet was not a bad idea. Maybe Nora needed a puppy. Or a kitten. Or a prairie dog.

"But what if she doesn't wish for it?" Isabelle pressed Clotilda. "What if she doesn't want anything I can give her?"

"That's not possible." Clotilda rolled her eyes. "If you don't believe me, check the appendix to Rule Twenty-Seven." It was the rule for matching a princess with a godmother in training:

Fairy godmothers in training are matched with practice princesses (or otherwise) with the following qualifications:

    a)   They have made a wish that will make them happy if fulfilled.

b) They know someone who has made a wish on their behalf.

c) They believe deeply in the power of magic.

d) any of the above

e) all of the above

As far as Isabelle could tell, Nora was none of the above. But she didn't say that to Clotilda.

Instead, she walked back to her room and flopped on her bed and felt sorry for herself. This was what she deserved: a serious regular girl who didn't want anything she could give her.

Isabelle didn't know what to do. She didn't want to lose her sparkles. She didn't want to be the worst in the class. She didn't want to be like Mom.

Late that night, when she couldn't sleep, she crept back to the girlgoyles. She swooshed her wand and held it up to the starry sky. She shouted, "I can do this! I am going to be a great fairy godmother. I am going to figure out what will make Nora happily ever after. And then I'm going to give it to her."

Then she waited for some kind of magical sign.

Unfortunately, only the girlgoyles heard her. And they couldn't help or give her any advice. After all, they really were just made of rock.

Chapter Eleven

The Worst Princess Makes Her Wish...
Sort Of

The next day, on the first day of the third week, Isabelle went back to the spyglass.

It was a slow, sleepy Saturday. Isabelle didn't expect anything to happen.

Nora was sitting at the window watching a cute bunny hop around her backyard. She opened her window and tossed it a carrot. Then she yawned without covering her mouth. She made a sound like "Aaaaaah-waaaaah," which was really just a very loud yawn, but Isabelle strained her ears and imagined that if she had a cold—which was technically possible—"Aaaaa-waaaah" could actually be "I wish."

Isabelle seized the moment.

She didn't care that she was supposed to wait for the exact right moment, or that she was supposed to foster independence in her practice princess.

Nora was not a usual princess. She was a regular girl. Isabelle wasn't going to follow even the few rules she knew.

She put as many sparkles as possible on the tip of her thumb. Then she pinched them as hard as she could and held her wand high. She swished and she twirled. For luck, she crossed her fingers. She was pretty sure she needed it.

And then she did it. She felt herself go and be transported to Nora. It was the best feeling ever. Not exactly like flying. More like flying at supersonic speed until everything stopped and you were somewhere else and it was really hard to control yourself and not jump up and down in the sparkle dust.

Sparkles were really messy. First, they floated up to the ceiling. Then, just when the air began to feel clear, they turned into dust and drifted down to the floor until everything in the room—every trophy, notebook, and pillow—looked shiny and slippery. In a way, sparkle dust resembled tree pollen—or a whole field of dandelions exploding at once. When it had settled, everything looked slightly fuzzy.

Isabelle smiled at the speechless, shocked girl who stood in front of her. She waved her wand back and forth the way she'd seen Clotilda do. Then she said the words she'd dreamed of saying since before she'd even passed her training:

"Hello, Nora. I am your fairy godmother. I'm here to make your wish come true!"

Chapter Twelve

The Things You Can't Wish For

Nora looked one-third disgusted, one-third amused, and one-third in need of a shower and a stretch. The first thing she did was run to the door. "Help! Someone! Police!"

Isabelle would've run after her, but she had a sparkle stuck in her throat. So instead, she coughed until Nora stopped shouting and brought her a glass of water and a long list of very obvious questions.

"Who are you, really? Why are you here? How did you get here? What do you want from me?"

Isabelle was only too happy to answer. "Like I said, I'm your fairy godmother. I'm here to grant your wish and make you happily ever after! Just name it, and you've got it."

Hearing this, Nora should have felt like dancing, too. But she didn't. She crossed her arms over her chest. She looked suspicious. "But I didn't make any wishes."

Of course, Isabelle knew this, but she wasn't going to admit it.

"Yes you did."

"No I didn't."

"Yes you did."

"No I didn't."

This was not going well at all. "Fine. You didn't. But since I'm here, you must want something." When Nora stayed silent, Isabelle had to think fast. "I could make you a rabbit," she said. She pointed her wand at the stuffed animals on top of Nora's bed. "I know for a fact that you thought that bunny outside was super cute."

Isabelle flicked her wrist and swooshed around in a half twirl. She prayed that something would happen.

At first, nothing happened. It was a little embarrassing.

So she raised her wand higher and thought very hard about pets and how great it was to have one. She thought about that rabbit outside, and how sad Nora must be because she couldn't go outside and pet it. And then she looked at Nora, and she wanted her to be happy. For a split second, Isabelle could feel that Nora wanted to believe.

A white bunny appeared on Nora's bed in a small cloud of white sparkles. It was a small one. But it was real. And fluffy. And when it twitched its nose, it looked very cute.

"Ta-da!" Isabelle cried. "Aren't you happy now?"

To Isabelle's surprise, Nora did not clap her hands. She did not look even mildly happy. Her eyes started to water.

Her skin changed from pale to pink to this blotchy red that was very unbecoming and un-princess-like. If that wasn't bad enough, she began to scratch her arms and legs and fingers and head. Then the sneezing started.

Between sneezes, Nora managed to say, "Get that thing out of here. I'm allergic!"

"Sorry!" Isabelle raised her wand to use some magic, but then she stopped. She didn't want to risk messing up a second time. Plus, she was already low on sparkles. Instead, she chased the bunny around the room until it was so tired it let her pick it up and take it outside.

When she came back, Nora was almost done vacuuming. Her skin looked back to normal. She only sneezed a few more times.

"So maybe you don't want a pet," Isabelle said. "But there must be some other kind of wish I can grant for you."

Nora didn't say anything at first. "Okay then, Fairy Godmother. I thought about it, and I know what I want. I would like to wish for world peace!"

Isabelle didn't know what to say. "World peace? I can't make that."

Nora tried to hide her disappointment. "What about clean air, then?" When Isabelle shook her head no, Nora paced around her room. Suddenly, she snapped her fingers. "How about clean water for everyone in the world? Or no, I've got something better. Let's end world hunger."

Isabelle lowered her wand. She sat down on Nora's bed.

Nora said, "Can you possibly make mean people nice? Or, even better—turn them into frogs?"

Although this sounded like a really excellent idea, Isabelle knew she couldn't pull that off, either. She wasn't even sure she wanted to. "I'm sorry," she said, "but I can't do any of those things."

This was getting really awkward.

Isabelle explained one of the few things she knew for sure: that fairy godmother magic was limited and that personal happiness was the key to successful wish granting.

"Do you have a piece of fruit? Maybe a peach or a nectarine? If it's a little bit ripe, I can probably make you a bike. Do you want two wheels or three?"

"I don't really need a bike." Nora frowned deeply.

Isabelle wiggled her feet to keep her toes from turning numb. "What about some amazing shoes?" She pointed to her own black-and-white shoes with silver-tipped pointed toes. They were hand-me-downs from Clotilda—cute, but a little tight. "Aren't these nice? If you want, I can make a pair just like them." Isabelle raised her wand again.

Nora shook her head. "I like the shoes I have." Isabelle checked them out. Sneakers. They looked worn in, and the laces were bright green.

Isabelle wouldn't want to trade those in, either. They looked pretty much perfect, like they'd be great for twirling.

But this was beside the point, and Isabelle knew it. Now that she was here, she had no time to waste. She had to make this visit count and grant Nora some kind of wish.

She didn't have *that* much time left before the deadline. But she couldn't admit that to Nora.

Isabelle wondered if she could scare her into wishing for something. "You know," she said in her most threatening voice, "if you can't think of anything to wish for, I could get my sister to put you in a deep sleep for a hundred years." Although she wasn't sure Clotilda would agree to do that, in theory it wasn't the worst idea ever. While Nora slept, Isabelle could go home and look in a book for suggestions on dealing with difficult princesses. But Clotilda probably wouldn't help. No doubt, there was a rule about that.

Nora lay down on her bed. "Fine with me. Go get your sister. I'll leave my family a note. You say a hundred years? This is going to be so amazing."

"Are you crazy?" Isabelle cried. The deep-sleep idea was supposed to be for emergencies only, and this was not an emergency. Or maybe it was . . .

Isabelle didn't know. She really didn't know anything.

She paced around the room. "There must be something that would make you happy right now, this second."

"As a matter of fact, there is," Nora said, finally smiling in a sort of sneaky (and un-princess-y) way. "I'd be very happy if you would leave."

Chapter Thirteen

No One Likes to Be Rejected

Over the next five days, things didn't get better. But they didn't get worse, either. Nora stayed serious. Isabelle stayed determined. She decided that the best place to hear her princess's wish was right next to Nora, whether Nora liked it or not!

When Isabelle showed up the sixth day, Nora said, "I think I'm going outside to pick up garbage," so Isabelle grabbed a garbage bag and walked around the park with her. This might sound sort of boring, but the sun was warm, and it turns out running around making things look nice was a lot of fun. People in the regular world were slobs! In just one afternoon, Isabelle and Nora picked up five bags of trash and two bags of glass bottles. When they brought them to the dump to be recycled, Nora didn't look happily ever after yet, but her good mood was definitely encouraging.

So the day after that, when Nora wanted to collect clothes for the needy, Isabelle helped knock on doors. She was willing to magically repair the clothes, but there was no need. Nora was too fast. She sewed up every hole all by herself.

When Isabelle thought about it, Nora was not that different from a fairy godmother. She was just more practical and solved problems with her hands that Isabelle would have covered in sparkles.

"You might want to spend a little less time glued to your princess and a little bit more time planning," Clotilda said. "But don't ask me. I'm just your sister who landed one of the best princesses ever. What do I know?"

She wasn't joking.

Three more days passed. Isabelle and Nora made lemonade for Nora's stepbrother and his friends. They recycled plastic bottles. They saved a caterpillar from getting squashed on the sidewalk. Isabelle was having so much fun with Nora, she almost forgot she was a fairy godmother on a deadline.

Grandmomma, however, was on top of things. Every night, when Isabelle returned from Nora's house, Grandmomma pointed to the calendar and asked, "Do you have any progress to report?"

Unfortunately, all Isabelle had were hopes and excuses. It apparently wasn't going to be enough to spend time with Nora. She had to do something more—something she didn't want to do.

She had to ask for help.

She knocked on Clotilda's door.

"Is it okay if I talk to the brother?" she asked Clotilda, after Clotilda ushered her inside.

"That would be highly unusual," Clotilda said, but that wasn't the same as no. This technicality gave Isabelle a sliver of hope. She was sure she was on the right track.

Even though he was young (and a boy), Gregory practically worshipped his stepsister. Before Clotilda could change her mind and alert Grandmomma to a possible problem, Isabelle grabbed a couple of sparkles and made her way to Nora's house.

Travel was getting easier. This time, she hardly left more than a sprinkling of sparkle dust on the kitchen floor.

"Bella," Gregory said when he saw her. "Stand next to me. We're making purple macarons!" Gregory and his mother were nice people with big imaginations, but not big enough to believe in magic or wishes or fairy godmothers. It didn't matter how many times Nora told them who Isabelle was. They thought she was just a girl who was new to the neighborhood. They didn't seem to notice that she never knocked. Or that she had a knack for showing up right before treats were about to come out of the oven.

As they put the cookies on cooling racks, Mrs. Silverstein sang. During cleanup, she danced with the broom. She acted almost exactly like an old-fashioned storybook princess. Only she made her purple macarons with food coloring, not with the help of cheerful mice.

After she was done, Nora's stepmom turned to Isabelle. "Would it make you happy if I packed some of these up so the three of you could go to the park and eat them?"

No one had ever asked Isabelle what would make her happy. "What about Nora? Would that make her happy?" Isabelle asked.

"It would make her very happy," Gregory said.

Isabelle ran into Nora's room to get her. "Your stepmom made cookies. And they look amazing. You want to take some to the park to eat?"

Nora did not look happy. "Not today," she said. And she was serious about it.

"What's the matter?" Isabelle asked. "Did something happen?"

"I just don't want to go to the park," Nora said. "What if we stay here and the two of us climb a tree instead?"

Isabelle understood. Having a little brother was probably almost as annoying as having a bossy older sister. The girls collected their cookies and headed out to Nora's backyard.

Sitting in Nora's tree was almost as perfect as sitting between the girlgoyles. The tree had a thick trunk and many strong branches perfect for sitting. Isabelle noticed a bunch of initials, hearts, and flowers carved into the strongest branch. "Are those from your friends?" Isabelle asked, but Nora must not have heard her.

"Look over there," Isabelle said, pointing toward the highest leaves. "It's a nest."

When Nora's back was turned, Isabelle waved her wand, and a baby robin peeked its head out and flew onto Nora's outstretched hand.

"It's so cute," Nora said with a huge smile on her face.

For the first time, Isabelle noticed that Nora had a dimple.

"Did you do that?" Nora asked. "Did you make that happen?"

This was the kind of thing that happened to lots of real princesses (not regular girls) in stories, but Isabelle refused to take any credit. She remembered what Grandmomma had said about giving your princess independence, and how Raine had grown powerful without taking credit for her magic. "Not my expertise," she said with a shrug. "What do you want to do next?"

"Let's climb down and see if Gregory wants to play a game," Nora suggested.

On the ground, Isabelle taught them how to play the trust game. She still didn't think it was really a game, but she was sure they both would like it. It was sort of fun to fall into each other's arms. After they had each taken a turn, Gregory demanded another round. So first, Nora caught Gregory. Then Isabelle caught Gregory. Then Nora caught Gregory again. Gregory would have fallen ten more times, but Nora wanted to show Isabelle something secret inside—without her younger brother tagging along.

They went inside and upstairs to her room. Nora crawled under her bed and came out with an old wooden box that had a smooth top and a silver lock on one side. Isabelle was pretty sure Nora had never shown it to anyone before.

"It belonged to my mother. My real one," Nora said.

Isabelle understood how important this must be. "What's in it?"

"Just little things that she liked." There was a porcelain cat, a baseball cap, and a couple of paintbrushes in the box.

"I bet she was nice," Isabelle said, holding a picture of someone who looked a lot like Nora, only older.

Nora nodded. "She was the best mother in the whole world."

Isabelle thought about her own mother and how much she wished she had a picture or a box of mementos.

"In the beginning, I thought all of this fairy godmother stuff was a little silly," Nora confessed. "But you're nice.

And hanging out has been really fun. And not that silly at all."

Isabelle smiled. "And I really wish I could make world peace for you. Or clean air. Or end poverty."

Nora might not be like any of the other godmothers' princesses, but Isabelle was happy about the way things were going. Nora was right—those things would make the world (and the fairy godmother world, too) a happier place. Being serious was not the same thing as being sad.

Plus, there were snacks at Nora's house.

"Would you like me to make you a picture of the fairy godmother world?" Isabelle asked. She wanted to share everything with Nora.

When Nora nodded, Isabelle whipped out her wand and began to show off. With one flick, she painted a map of the entire fairy godmother world. With another, she filled the northern part with giant yellow flowers and green-and-pink trees that reminded her of Angelica. For the southern part, she tapped her wand to make light-blue clouds and soft waves for Fawn. And in the middle, she flicked her wrist a few times to make the fields and the lakes and the perfect sunny days that she had lived in all her life. She even had enough sparkle power to make the castles and her secret hiding place. And, of course, the girlgoyles.

She wanted Nora to love them as much as she did. "They're beautiful," Isabelle said. She wished Nora could see them. "They're my best friends."

Nora didn't smile. The truth was she looked a little strange. But maybe she was just thinking about her real mom. "You would totally love them," Isabelle continued, waving her wand to give the girlgoyles a little extra pizzazz. "You can see everything when you sit right between them."

Nora didn't look at the painting. She didn't look like she wished she could sit there. "I don't get what's so special about them. They're not alive. They can't talk. They don't do anything."

Even though everything Nora said was technically true, her words still stung.

Isabelle stopped painting. Something was wrong. It was something Isabelle hoped she could fix. But she didn't know exactly what to say. Or do. So she sat still and listened.

Nora said, "There's a place I know that's even better than my tree or your girlgoyles. It's beautiful. And no one goes there but me. If you want, I'll take you there tomorrow. Unless you like having blisters, magic yourself a good pair of shoes."

She's taking me to her special woods! Isabelle thought to herself.

Later that night, Isabelle sat with the girlgoyles. She tested out the new shoes she'd made for the next day's hike. She even thought about opening the rule book.

But she was confident Grandmomma had taught her everything she needed to know:

- Nora deserved happiness.

- Wishes were never granted by magic alone.

- Happily ever after shouldn't be that hard.

She also knew she shouldn't have visited Nora before she made a real wish. She'd visited her way more than she was supposed to.

There was only one thing she could do now. Even though she was pretty sure she was doing exactly what her mother would have done, she would keep visiting Nora. At this rate, she had nothing to lose. Nora knew what she could do. She knew what she couldn't do. Either she made her wish now, or she wasn't going to ever make a wish.

Isabelle knew what that meant.

No sparkles. No wand. No Extravaganza.

She'd be the worst fairy godmother ever. Even worse than her mother.

Chapter Fourteen

Rock Scrambles and a Rock with a View

The next day, Isabelle was ready.

Together, she and Nora headed down the street and into the wooded area by Nora's house. Nora climbed the path quickly, and Isabelle tried her best to keep up. Nora jumped from rock to rock like she was the one with magical powers.

"It's just a few minutes longer," Nora said. "And just a little bit higher."

They walked around tall green trees and patches of wildflowers and even a tiny stream that was ice-cold and crystal clear.

"It's beautiful here," Isabelle said.

"Just wait," Nora said.

Nora pointed to a big patch of blue sky and a very small clearing. In the center was a huge rock big enough to seat two or maybe even three people. Isabelle sat down next to Nora. "This is unbelievable." The clearing was almost as perfect as her fairy godmother world. "That rock scramble was awesome."

"And so was jumping over the creek," Nora added.

Isabelle laughed. "Yes! I also liked how you tagged the trees, like you were running a race. I like to do that, too."

Nora grinned. "See! I told you this would be better than hanging out with those girlgoyles."

Instead of making a fuss, Isabelle thought about how to make the moment better. She pointed her wand at Nora's backpack. "Are you hungry?" With a quick flick of her wrist, Isabelle directed a small puff of sparkles at the backpack.

When Nora opened her bag, she found cheeses and breads and chocolates and peaches. "This is perfect! How did you know I was starting to feel hungry?"

Together, they arranged all the snacks on the rock. "This is every one of my favorite foods! Everything except for ice cream!"

Together they ate all the treats that Isabelle had poofed into the backpack. They also played cards and admired the view. They picked up pretty rocks and leaves and flowers for Nora's stepmother, and then they looked for salamanders. Nora found hers first. She wondered, for just a moment, if Isabelle could turn him into a horse. (She couldn't. Not yet, anyway . . .)

Nora put her hands together. "There's something I've been meaning to ask you." She took a deep breath.

This is it. The wish. Isabelle gripped her wand.

She could already picture herself at the Extravaganza.

"I wish . . . I wish you didn't have to leave," Nora said. "Or that I could come visit you." She got really excited. "Or even better, I wish I could live in the fairy godmother world with you. Then I could run around the fields with you and we could go to the wild place with plants. And we could hop from cloud to cloud, and maybe I could learn to grant wishes, too."

This was a nice sentiment, but regular girls were not allowed to visit the fairy godmother world—Isabelle was sure of that. "I'm sorry," Isabelle said. (And she really was.) "I wish we could do that, too, but it isn't possible. I don't get my own wishes. I just get to grant them. I have to follow the rules."

Nora nodded like she understood, but now she looked a little less happy.

This was a problem.

"Then how about I wish for more wishes? Like maybe a thousand wishes?" Nora said. But she was smart. The second she said it, she took it back. "I guess that's against the rules, too?"

Isabelle thought they'd been over this rule before. Hadn't Nora been listening? "The other godmothers were done right away," she grumbled. "Even Minerva. And she's really old." Before she could stop herself, she added, "I'll never make it to Level Two at this rate!"

Nora dropped the salamander she'd been holding. (Don't worry. He was fine.) A curious expression came over her face.

"Now I get it," she said. "Helping me is some kind of test. And if you pass, you get to get rid of me, right?"

Isabelle tried to deny it, but it was sort of true. "That's not exactly how this works." She wasn't sure how to explain the rules without breaking some kind of fairy godmother code or hurting Nora's feelings.

"So it is a test." Nora stood up and took a step away from Isabelle. "You're no better than all the girls in my class."

She began to pack up the backpack as fast as she could. "What do I have to do so you can go back to the other godmothers and your precious girlgoyles that can't even do anything? Because I'll do it. I'll do it right now." When Isabelle didn't move, she started walking away. "You know, I was just fine before you showed up. Why don't you just leave me alone?"

Then she took off down the trail. Fast.

Isabelle slumped down on the rock and watched Nora disappear. She had messed up big-time. And now there was only one thing she could do.

Chapter Fifteen

Flattery Will Get You Everywhere

*B*ack in her room, Isabelle prepared to grovel. She brushed her hair and pulled on her nicest skirt. She ripped the plastic wrapping off her fairy godmother books, gathered them up, and walked down the hall until she stood in front of her sister's door. Then she knocked. "Are you in there, sweetest, smartest, most wonderful, most beautiful, greatest fairy godmother ever?" Flattery worked on Clotilda. "Can I ask you a question? It's really very important."

Clotilda opened her door and told her to sit down. "I'm sorry," she said. "I saw everything through the spyglass. Grandmomma can't say you didn't try."

"Try" was one way to put this total disaster of a day.

Isabelle refused to let her sister see her cry. "Nora's miserable! And it's because of me." She steadied her chin in what she considered a brave sort of way. "And don't tell me it's because she's a regular girl. It's not! She's just serious. But she's good, too. And nice. She wants to make the world a better place. She deserves to be happy."

Clotilda dabbed her eye with a hankie. "That is just so beautiful, Isabelle. I didn't think it was possible, but you have come to care about your regular girl."

Isabelle wished she'd stop calling Nora a regular girl. Nora was not regular. But now wasn't the time. "The problem is she doesn't know what she wants to wish for," she said in her sweetest voice possible. "What would you have done for Melody if she hadn't known?"

Now Clotilda looked confused. "I don't understand."

"I mean, what would you have done if Melody had wished for something you couldn't grant?" When she saw that Clotilda didn't think this was possible, she added, "Hypothetically, of course. That would never happen to you, since you are such an amazing fairy godmother and would never get stuck in a total pickle like me."

Clotilda still looked puzzled, but Isabelle could see she appreciated the compliment. "You must be overthinking this. Grandmomma would never have given you a practice princess you couldn't make happy."

Isabelle agreed with this in theory. "And yet, even though I've visited her way too many times, she hasn't wished for anything that I can make come true."

Clotilda patted her on the back. "Well, you must be overlooking something. That's all there is to it," she said. "Have you looked in the Wish List? Or your rule book?"

Isabelle had to come clean. "I never read the book," she mumbled.

Clotilda shook her head but didn't look surprised. "Didn't I warn you . . ." she started to say, but then (thankfully) she stopped. "Well then, we can't worry about that now. All that matters is that you are smart and strong and care about Nora. And you don't have a lot of time. Tell me everything about her. There has to be something you're missing."

As Isabelle described Nora and everything they'd done, Clotilda rifled through the book. Isabelle hoped there was a chapter on unusual princesses. Or princesses who liked nature but didn't care about dresses. Or fairy godmothers who didn't read the book and still made it through training.

Then Isabelle remembered Nora's box. And the picture of her mother. And she felt even worse, if that was possible.

"What's the point of pretending? I'm just like Mom. I might as well give up now and turn in my wand."

"Over my perfect princess." Clotilda clamped her hand over Isabelle's mouth until she promised to be quiet. "Listen, I should have told you this before, but our mother was not all bad. Even when that stupid princess wasn't happy, she kept trying. She loved her almost as much as she loved us. If you're like her, that's a good thing. And she would be very proud of you right now."

It was the sappiest, nicest thing Clotilda had ever said!

Clotilda peeked outside her bedroom door to make sure Grandmomma wasn't snooping around. "Let's start from the beginning. What have you tried so far?"

Isabelle told her about the rabbit. And the questions. "You can't just tell me what to do?"

"Sorry."

"She's really mad."

Clotilda did not agree. "Are you sure? Did she tell you never to come back?"

"No."

"Then she's not mad. She's just hurt. And in the regular world, that means she wants you to come back and try again. And that means there's still hope. Give her a little time to cool down, then bright and early tomorrow show up and apologize. Forget about the Extravaganza for now. And this time, focus. Listen to her. You're my little sister, and I know you can fix this!"

Chapter Sixteen

Starry Night

That night, Isabelle climbed the tower to sit with the girlgoyles. She looked out at the star-filled sky and the bright moon. Tonight, the moon looked like a crescent.

She loved this place. Her whole life, she had wanted to be a real fairy godmother.

But now she wanted something more than that.

She wanted Nora to be happily ever after. If she couldn't make that happen in time, it didn't matter. If she didn't pass Level One and couldn't go to the Extravaganza, she could deal with it. As long as Nora got what she wanted.

She whispered, "What should I do?" and "Are you out there?" Then a little louder, "Do you see me?"

And then she stood very still and listened. For a moment, she thought she heard her name. It sounded like the voice she'd been longing to hear her entire life. Her mother's voice.

Isabelle didn't move.

At first, the voice felt very far away. Like a whisper. But then it got louder, until she could understand what was actually happening. It wasn't her mother; it was Nora.

Nora was making a wish!

Isabelle turned to the girlgoyles. "I know how to make Nora happy. I know what she wants!"

Of course, the girlgoyles said nothing. But it didn't matter. Isabelle didn't need their advice.

Nora was not the kind of girl who wanted simple things, like a dress or a bike or even sparkly shoes. She was way too young for a crush. She had been so busy saving the world, she never took the time to wish for herself.

And that was a good thing—mostly because Isabelle couldn't even turn fruit into a strawberry hot-fudge sundae (Nora's favorite). She had to be honest about that.

But now that didn't matter.

Nora had made her wish. And Isabelle had heard her. Loud and clear. Tomorrow, Isabelle was going to make Nora happily ever after.

She held the girlgoyles' hands and hugged them like they were real. "Wish me luck."

Chapter Seventeen

Hurt Feelings and Wishes

The next day, Isabelle arrived at Nora's house earlier than usual.

She found her stepmother in the kitchen. She was making bread with white chocolate and apricots. "Would you like a slice?" she asked.

"I would love one."

Mrs. Silverstein smiled. She was still humming and singing and dancing around the kitchen like an old-fashioned storybook princess.

"Did you and Nora have a fight?" Nora's stepmother asked.

Isabelle nodded. She had to admit it was one she didn't fully understand. "I think I hurt her feelings. Did she tell you anything about it?"

Nora's stepmom wouldn't explain. "If she wants you to know, she'll tell you." (This made her a very good stepmother, but not very useful to Isabelle.)

Isabelle knew she had to act fast. "Did she go back to the woods?"

Mrs. Silverstein handed her three pieces of bread. "Actually, I asked her to take her brother to the park."

As Isabelle opened the door, Nora's stepmother said, "Good luck, Isabelle! Whatever Nora said, I'm sure she didn't mean it. You are a good friend. Just the kind I wished Nora would meet."

Isabelle stopped in her tracks. "Wished for?" she repeated.

Nora's stepmom nodded. "I actually did. On a shooting star! It sounds a little silly to say out loud, but when I saw it, I couldn't resist."

"Not silly at all," Isabelle whispered. Everything began to fall into place for Isabelle. A shooting star wish was very old, very powerful magic.

When Isabelle got to the park, it was full of people. Gregory was playing on the curly slide. Nora was sitting under a tree with her arms crossed over her chest.

She was alone. She looked miserable.

Isabelle sat down next to her. She was going to say something, but then a few girls wandered over to say hello. They wanted to know who Isabelle was and what she was doing there.

Nora didn't look happy to see Isabelle. "She's my lousy fairy godmother."

This made the girls laugh, like Nora had made a hilarious joke. "No really, are you cousins? Why don't you come and hang out with us? We're going to walk to the library."

Even though Isabelle was a little insulted—she thought all girls believed in fairy godmothers—she saw this moment as a big opportunity. "Sure," she said, jumping up, but Nora turned stiff as a girlgoyle.

"Go ahead. Have a grand time." Nora sat there with her arms still crossed and her fists balled up. "But I'm going to stay here."

Isabelle told the girls they'd see them later. "What's the matter?" she asked Nora, sitting back down. "Those girls didn't seem that bad. In fact, they seemed pretty nice."

Nora didn't want to explain. "I said you can go without me if you want. Maybe you can grant their wishes and get your promotion. Maybe they'll be almost as fun as your girlgoyles."

Isabelle sat down. She had a lot of important things to say. "First of all, I'm sorry," she told Nora. "I acted like you were a test question, and you're not. You think I don't want to be friends with you, but I do."

Nora nodded, but she still looked mad. Or maybe sad. She got up and brushed herself off and told her brother they were leaving. "I just want to go home. If you want to find someone else, it's okay with me."

Isabelle followed her. She was not about to give up now. She said, "You can't get rid of me." And "You can tell me anything." And "I was so happy when you showed me the box."

As they walked, Isabelle picked up some cans. Gregory found ten pennies and a lizard. Nora looked down at the ground. She didn't pick up any garbage. She didn't say anything until they got home.

They climbed the tree so they could talk in total privacy. "Those girls used to be my best friends," Nora said finally. "They used to come to my house every single day. We took hikes together. We ate snacks together. But then one day, something changed. I still don't know what. One day, we were climbing my tree. The next day, they cared about other things. They didn't want to talk to me. That's why I got so mad when you told me about the girlgoyles."

Isabelle now understood why she was sent here. She had seen it the very first time she watched Nora through the spyglass.

But this was not the time to talk. This was a time to listen.

Nora continued, "When you were talking about the girlgoyles, I got jealous. I thought you were going to dump me, like they did." She took a deep breath, because it was clear that what she was about to say took guts. "But last night, I realized three things. The first is that I trust you, and I'm sorry I acted that way. The second is I believe in magic. But the third is that I don't want it. I don't need it. Not now. Not ever."

Isabelle wanted to twirl (but she didn't; she was in a tree). She also wanted to tell Nora that she wasn't all that confident about her magic anyway. And that Nora's stepmother had already made a wish for her. But she didn't, in case telling her was against the rules.

Nora said, "I have always wanted a friend who cares about the world—a friend who likes cooking and hiking, like me. But most of all, I want a friend who won't leave."

She looked really serious.

"I get that you're a fairy godmother and you have other people to help. I'm just not ready to say good-bye yet."

Isabelle knew how hard it was to feel alone. She definitely understood missing her mother. She knew what it felt like to have a wish that couldn't be granted.

"So last night," Nora said, "I wished that you didn't have to be my fairy godmother anymore. I know it's silly, but I just want you to come over sometimes. Maybe even stay overnight. I wished that we could just be friends."

They climbed down the tree. Isabelle took out her wand, but she didn't need it. She was 99.9 percent sure that she could still be a fairy godmother while being friends with people in the regular world.

If there was ever a moment for *all of the above*, this was it. Nora didn't need magic. She didn't need tricks. She needed a friend. In this case, she needed a friend who was also a fairy godmother.

Chapter Eighteen

Granting Wishes Just in Time

Isabelle did her half twirl and her swoosh—just for fun.

She said, "Your wish has been granted. We will be friends. No matter what!"

Then she gave Nora a huge hug. Then they went into the house and gave Nora's stepmom a huge hug. They hugged Gregory, too—not that he really understood why.

Nora was feeling almost as sappy as Isabelle. "For a long time," she said, "I stopped wishing for a best friend."

She stood taller. "Then you showed up, and I knew I had found one."

The irony was obvious.

Isabelle and Nora were already friends, and Isabelle had already made her happy. Now they needed to figure out the *ever after* part.

Obviously, they started with snacks.

They ate two sundaes and also some cookies and some of that bread that Nora's stepmom had just made. Even though bread didn't technically go with the rest of the snacks, it was warm and delicious. Especially with a spoonful of honey on top.

When people are happily ever after, they don't worry about silly things like matching food.

Isabelle might have hung out there all night, but about midway through the second sundae, her stomach started to feel strange.

This time it wasn't because she had done anything wrong.

It was someone (or something) tugging at her. Like a clock.

"The Extravaganza!" Isabelle cried. "I forgot! I need to go home and get ready."

When Nora looked confused, Isabelle made her promise to wait up. "I'll be back as soon as I can. I'll tell you everything later."

Back at the castle, Isabelle found Clotilda in Grandmomma's office. Both of them had their feet up on the desk.

"Right under the wire, just like I told you," Clotilda said, holding out her hand for a large envelope, probably full of sparkles.

Isabelle was too happy to be mad. "You bet against me?" she said to Grandmomma. She couldn't believe it. She turned to Clotilda. "You bet with me?"

Grandmomma put her feet on the ground and smoothed out her dress. "What was I supposed to do? You never read the books. You didn't even pretend to read the contract. All that fine print—you think I made that up for my health?"

Isabelle waited for her to mention other things. Like the stolen sparkles. And the spyglass. But she didn't.

"So, yes, I bet against you." She almost smiled. "But I'm glad I lost."

Clotilda peeked in the envelope. (She was really enjoying this.) "I told her you had it in the bag." She patted Grandmomma on the back. "She was the right princess at the right time. Just like you always say."

Grandmomma nodded. "But you took such a long time."

Clotilda agreed. "We kept waiting for you to find her a friend. But you ended up *becoming* her friend instead. It was sort of charming. A real happily ever after. Just like it should be."

"That is *true*," Grandmomma said. She picked up a picture of Nora. Unlike in the first one, now she was smiling. "But you could have made it a lot easier on yourself.

Why do you think I made you play the trust game? How many times did I have to tell you that there is no purpose more important than helping others achieve their happily ever after? Or that happily ever after isn't only about magic? Or that the magic didn't come just from sparkles?"

If there was one thing Grandmomma liked to say, it was "I told you so." Also "I was right." And "How many times did I have to tell you?" Today she finished with "You really should have read the books. The fine print is not that fine."

Clotilda agreed. "After the Extravaganza, I'll help you review."

Even though this was technically a very good idea, Isabelle didn't want to think about the rules. She wanted to go back and visit Nora. (She didn't tell Clotilda that. It would have hurt her feelings.) Grandmomma handed her a book. "Can you read Rule Ten out loud?"

Isabelle looked at the writing. "Can you turn on a light? The letters look fuzzy."

"Fuzzy, you say?" Now Clotilda handed Grandmomma an envelope—probably full of sparkles. "Meaning you can't read it?"

"Yes. Fuzzy." She'd never thought about it before. "What is going on?"

"Grandmomma thinks you need glasses." (The fine print was, in fact, not that fine.)

Isabelle put the book down. "You can't just wave your wand and make them better?"

Grandmomma looked a bit sheepish. "Sorry. Not everything can be solved with magic."

Tomorrow there'd be plenty of time to check her eyes and order some glasses. Right now, they had to get ready for the Extravaganza.

Grandmomma waved her wand and turned Isabelle's regular clothes into a pretty orange-and-purple dress, complete with new shoes and a fancy hairstyle. Isabelle twirled one time—without knocking anything over. She admired her bright green sparkly sneakers—a little worn in. It was a nice touch. She knew Nora would approve.

"Ready?" Clotilda said. (In the fairy godmother world, there was no such thing as fashionably late. *Fashionably late* was another way of saying *rude*. Especially when it came to the Extravaganza, everyone showed up on time.)

"Ready," Isabelle said. A few sparkles flew in the air. She couldn't stop herself. She needed one more spin.

For once, Grandmomma did not object. "You did it! And now, it's party time."

Chapter Nineteen

There's Nothing Better
Than a Big Old Party

In the fairy godmother world, just like the regular one, there was nothing better than a big old fancy party, especially if the decorations were sparkly and the food was delicious.

And the food at the Extravaganza was supposed to be out of this world.

"I will never forget the first time I walked up these steps," Clotilda said to Isabelle in her extremely cheerful voice, the one she always used when other fairy godmothers might be listening. "When you walk into the parlor, don't rush. Stop and look around. The Bests always make sure that every detail is covered."

Clotilda wasn't kidding. The parlor was so gigantic, Isabelle needed to stop and take a breath so she didn't feel dizzy. From floor to ceiling, every ounce of it glimmered and shimmered and glowed. The ceiling glittered like a star-filled sky. The floor felt dry, but Isabelle almost jumped back—it looked like raging water. The walls were covered with jewels and mirrors, and in every corner and on every wall, there were girlgoyles—except these girls were painted in all kinds of bright colors. To Isabelle, they looked like they were cheering for her.

"So what do we do first?" Isabelle asked Clotilda.

"Mingle, of course." Clotilda seemed to know everyone in the room already. "Why don't you go find your friends and give them your good news?"

Isabelle scanned the room until she found Angelica and Fawn. They were standing with some fairy godmothers who looked a lot like them, only older and slightly more wrinkly. "Hello," Isabelle said. She smiled at Angelica. "How was the Mediterranean? How did you grant your princess's wish to sail a ship?"

"It was easy peasy," Angelica said. "All I did was enter her name in a contest to win a sailing course and voila! She loved the boat. Last time I checked, she was talking about sailing around the world with her parents."

Fawn was slightly less boastful. "Mine was very sweet. And very young. When she saw snow for the first time, she couldn't stop laughing. She even built a snow godmother!"

Isabelle wanted to tell them about Nora, but the only questions they asked Isabelle were about Melody—not Nora. "Did you get to watch your sister work? Do you think Melody will find love one day? Or will she want to go to another rodeo?" Any other day, this might have made Isabelle feel bad, but today she didn't care. They were at the Extravaganza. Nora was happy. The food looked great.

She loved her green sparkly sneakers. When some older godmothers formed a conga line, Isabelle jumped to the front and weaved them around the tables and chairs until it was time to sit down.

Isabelle found her assigned seat in the very back corner of the room, near the bathroom.

Minerva was there. So were Irene and MaryEllen and a couple of older fairy godmothers who were close to the Worst, but not there yet.

Of course, they were complaining.

They didn't like the food.

The music was too loud.

They thought that all the young godmothers were overdressed.

Minerva pointed to Angelica and Fawn. They were seated next to the Bests. "We told you it was rigged."

"You think that's bad? My own grandmomma bet against me granting my princess's wish." She laughed it off. "What did your practice princesses want?"

Irene rolled her eyes. "New ballet slippers, of all things. For a recital she wasn't supposed to be able to dance in."

"A lost kitten who'd run away," MaryEllen said. She shrugged. "In the old days, the wishes were a lot juicier."

"It used to be that everyone wanted love," Minerva told Isabelle. "There were also evil witches. And no one had a phone. But now it's different. Some princesses want trips around the world. Some want their dream jobs. Some want to find love all by themselves!"

Secretly, Isabelle was relieved. "And some want to save the world. Or make a new friend."

Irene wondered if maybe it was time to retire. "The regular world just isn't what it used to be."

"I don't agree," Minerva said. "My practice princess was perfection. She was just like my first princess—a little bit wild, but always kind to animals." She took a bite of a little fried thing with mustard sauce on top. "And it was wonderful to be back in the Netherlands. The fields were blooming with flowers. I didn't need very many sparkles at all."

Isabelle smiled. She had never seen Minerva act so . . . happy.

Irene didn't look happy that Minerva was happy. "Was it hard for you to leave her?"

"It was excruciating," Minerva said. "So this morning, I filled out an official fairy godmother request form to save her for me when she becomes a real princess. I can wait that long to see her again."

Now Isabelle was a little confused. "Why did you have to request that?"

Minerva put her wrinkly hand on Isabelle's shoulder. She looked at her in a funny way. "Obviously, because practice princesses don't remember their fairy god-mothers. Don't tell me you forgot Rule Three C?"

When Isabelle said nothing, the Worsts all groaned. They knew the rule by heart.

Rule Three C: After the Extravaganza, all practice princesses will forget their fairy godmothers, no exceptions. This is because:

a) In the future, they may receive a new trainee.

b) They may someday receive a real fairy godmother.

c) If they don't forget, they might become lazy. They will tell their friends. And then everyone will want a fairy godmother and no one will want a trainee and fairy godmothers will stop being special.

Before they could get to *d*, Isabelle stopped them. "Do you mean *right* after the Extravaganza?"

This was terrible.

Isabelle got up and ran toward the podium. She had to fight for Nora.

Chapter Twenty

Rule Three C

$\mathcal{S}$he found Grandmomma talking to Number Five. "I need to speak to you about Rule Three C," Isabelle said.

Isabelle didn't wait for her to tell her it was also a rule she should have known. Or ask why she hadn't read it. Or why she'd only found out about it just now. "I don't care if it's a rule. It's not fair."

It's a sad fact that most rules do not work for everyone. Even if it's a good rule, it can be the wrong one for a few.

Grandmomma was not about to get into an argument at the Extravaganza. The truth was there wasn't much she could do. "Rules are rules. You signed on the line."

Isabelle wouldn't accept this. "But I promised Nora we would be friends forever. If she forgets me, it'll be like she never had one."

When people speak the truth, it is hard to argue, even when you are powerful and magical.

But Grandmomma was not like most people. Plus, she had anticipated this. She had written that rule for good reason. "Yes. I admit, it's a shame—what we call a vexing situation. But I can't make an exception for you. How would that look?"

Isabelle didn't care how it would look. Also, it sounded like Grandmomma was making an excuse.

"Listen," Grandmomma said, "think of it as simple economics. Supply and demand. Who would want to be a practice princess if you could wait and be a real princess later?"

That was true. But still not satisfying. "But Nora will be sad. That can't be right, either."

"She'll be no worse off than she was before she met you."

That was true, too.

"Forget about her," Grandmomma said. "This is about you. And your training. As I recall, you didn't think she was sad at all. Just serious." Now Grandmomma looked a bit smug. "If you want to be a good fairy godmother, you don't have a choice. Honestly, I told your mother the same thing."

Grandmomma had never spoken about Isabelle's mother like this before. "You did? Why?"

"You think I wanted my own daughter to be banished?" Grandmomma asked. "I told her to back off—to stop trying so hard and to leave the sparkles alone. That that princess wasn't worth it. But she wouldn't listen." She put both hands on Isabelle's shoulders. "But you're going to. Right?"

Isabelle took a step back.

If she wanted to stay friends with Nora, she didn't have much time.

"Okay," she told Grandmomma, crossing her fingers behind her back. "I will deal with it." As soon as she could, Isabelle turned and hurried out of the Extravaganza.

Back in her room, Isabelle felt something new. She couldn't be sure what to call it, but it seemed stronger than any magic she had ever felt before. Bigger than sparkles. Even bigger than a stepmother's wish on a shooting star. Isabelle was sure that something—or someone—was telling her to take a chance and do something quick.

It felt like she had her own fairy godmother—like someone was watching over her. Like maybe, no matter how far away she might be, her mother had not been completely banished.

Maybe she was still around. Somewhere.

Isabelle knew what she had to do. And she didn't have much time to spare.

Nora jumped when Isabelle arrived in a small, dusty cloud of sparkles. "What are you doing here? I thought you had to go to some party."

Isabelle tried not to talk too fast. "You have to listen. When you wake up tomorrow morning, you are not going to remember me."

Nora thought this was hilarious. "That's not true. We are friends for forever, just like I wished."

Isabelle didn't want to tell her that she hadn't read the fine print. But then she realized that she had to. "No. It's a rule. I'm sorry. I didn't read it. I didn't even open the rule book until it was too late."

Nora could have gotten mad, but it was really obvious that Isabelle was upset. "So why are you here? To say good-bye?" she asked quietly.

"No. I can't do that. I have a plan."

Isabelle took out the jar of sparkles she'd kept in her underwear drawer and put them gently on Nora's desk. "These are magic sparkles. I stole them from my grandmomma's office. I am going to leave them here with you. That way, if you need a friend, no matter where you are or what you're doing, you can find me."

Isabelle grabbed a piece of paper from Nora's desk and wrote:

How to use sparkles if you need a friend:

Take a pinch of them and throw a few in the air. Don't use a lot. They are more powerful than you understand.
So, I repeat: Don't use a lot.

Isabelle was sure that Nora, unlike her, would follow the rules. (Unlike Isabelle, she was a good student—and she also had very good eyesight.)

Then Isabelle put the sparkles where only Nora would see them: in her memory box—the one she kept under her bed. She gave Nora a huge hug.

"Trust me, you can have lots of friends. All those girls at the park? They want to be friends with you. I bet they don't understand what went wrong, either."

When Nora looked scared, Isabelle said, "It's going to be okay. You will forget me, but I'll never forget you. Even though it isn't in the rule book, I'll always be your fairy godmother."

Then she took a couple of sparkles out of the jar, pinched them between her thumb and her fingers, and in a puff, she disappeared.

Chapter Twenty-One

Happily Ever After Is More Than a Last Line

When Isabelle returned to the fairy godmother world, she did not go back to the Extravaganza, although she could hear that the party was in full swing. Right now, she didn't want to mingle with Angelica or Fawn. Or hear about their wonderful practice princesses. She didn't want to talk to Minerva. She definitely couldn't face Grandmomma or Clotilda. She wasn't even that hungry.

The one and only godmother she wanted to talk to was not here. But that was okay. Up until recently, she had been sure she'd never see her again.

But now, she wasn't so sure.

She was out there. Isabelle could feel it.

She climbed up the castle steps and outside to her secret hiding place. She sat in the cozy spot between the girlgoyles. The sky was particularly bright, just like it was supposed to be.

Already she missed Nora.

The girlgoyles seemed to understand. They always did.

Isabelle understood new things, too. She felt something she had never felt before. It was part confidence; part hope; part something else. She didn't know what to call it. Maybe gusto.

She felt ready for Level Two.

Also, she wouldn't admit this to Clotilda, but her sister was right. As soon as she got those glasses, she was going to read that book. Every single rule.

But mostly, Isabelle understood Mom. She knew why her mother had done everything she could to make her unhappy princess happy. She knew why she broke rules. She even understood why Grandmomma (with the emphasis on *momma*) had sent Isabelle to training and given her Nora instead of a princess who wanted a lost kitten.

Happily ever after was not just an ending. It was also the beginning. And a solid middle, too.

At least, she hoped so.

Just in case she was wrong, she made a wish. It was a complicated wish. (By now, she was used to complicated.) Isabelle wished that when Nora woke up in the morning:

> a) She would be happy. And she would stay happy. She would have vivid dreams about a fairy godmother who looked like a friend. She would realize that even without her, she could make new friends who liked to talk about important things.

b) If not, she would somehow find the sparkles. Also, she would follow the directions.

c) When she found the sparkles and followed the directions and threw some of them in the air, Isabelle would feel it. She would know Nora needed her. That was the connection between a fairy godmother and a princess, real or regular, that Isabelle finally understood.

Or, of course, there was always at least one more choice: *d) all of the above.* That kept her options open.

There was only one thing she hadn't considered. It was in the fine print.

Above all else, never give sparkles to anyone in the regular world!

Not a princess.

Not a mother.

Not anyone.

If you do, there will always be disaster.

You can count on it.

Acknowledgments

For a really long time, *The Wish List* was my "peach sorbet," my secret story that I pulled out when I was done with my "real" work and wanted to feel happy. I never meant to show it to anyone. I never thought I could write this kind of book. That it is now the first book in a series is proof of a) the power of play; b) writing without expectations; c) hard work, excellent friends, and a whole lot of magic; and of course, d) all of the above.

I'm so delighted to be able to thank all my fairy godmothers. I could not have done any of this without you.

All the sparkles to my editor, Anna Bloom, and the entire team at Scholastic Press. I am floored and humbled to work with all of you—and I still have to pinch myself that this is really happening. Heather Burns, thank you for making Isabelle and her girlgoyles come to life, right down to the sneakers. Of course, none of this would be happening without the support and gusto of my agent, Sarah Davies, who trusted me all the way—even when I was feeling "none of the above."

Thank you to Nancy Werlin, Amanda Jenkins, Nicole Valentine, Rob Costello, Jennifer Jacobson, and all the writers at the Highlights Whole Novel Workshop in 2014 who pushed me to share my peach sorbet and gave me the confidence to keep feeling it.

My dearest writer friends have been with me all the way. Special thanks to Tanya Lee Stone and Elly Swartz, Kathi Appelt, Tami Lewis Brown, Elle LaMarca, Micol Ostow, Kellye Carter Crocker, and Carmen Oliver. All of you read more drafts and took more phone calls and listened to more "what ifs" than friends are obliged to do. I'm convinced you all have wands!

My critique group in Evanston, Illinois, is more proof that magic is real. I am a better writer and reader because of Carolyn Crimi, Brenda Ferber, Jenny Meyerhoff, Laura Ruby, and Mary Loftus.

I am also lucky that so many writers trust me with their ideas and stories. In reading their work, I understand my own so much better. There aren't enough exclamation points to give to Mark Dahlby and all the writers.com writers, the VCFA Writing Novels for Young People Retreat, Melissa Fisher, the Highlights Foundation's Whole Novel Workshops, and Kent Brown, for trusting me with the best gigs ever! My family at Vermont College of Fine Arts grows every year, and I am so grateful for all your books and your enthusiasm and your tenacity. The SCBWI Work-in-Progress grant was my first indication that I might be able to make a go of this life. SCBWI continues to offer me amazing opportunities to learn and grow together (no *M* word)!

Thanks also to Alex, Ken, Bekki, Dian, Travis, Gail, Jeanette, Marilyn, Liz, Maria, and the rest of the CSD Department at Northwestern University. To Susan, Barb, Tina, Stephanie, Tzippy, Dianne, Kate, Fern, and Ashley: all of you taught me so much about teaching. Thank you for always being brave enough to give it right back to me!

I have never been all that concerned with the rules, but I couldn't even begin taking writing risks if my family didn't make me feel so safe and supported. Love to my parents, Judy and Rich, my sisters, Miriam and Annie, and everyone in my

Aronson and Klein families, especially Laura, Don, Ann, and Jon for sharing creativity and the arts from different points of view. Most important, my kids, Rebecca and Elliot: We will forever be the tripod! I would not be doing any of this without you and your love of books. To Ed, Liz, Anne, and Gregg: All of you inspire me—I just love where you're headed. Last, to my husband, Michael, who spends every day solving big problems in the real world while fostering the creativity and careers of so many people (and got me to ride my bike fast): The day we met will always be the best and luckiest day ever. That day, I definitely had a best fairy godmother looking out for me.

Happily ever after might not be the last line of every great story, but it is a wonderful feeling! Chocolate and flowers! I couldn't be more grateful.

About the Author

Sarah Aronson has always believed in magic—especially when it comes to writing. Her favorite things (in no particular order) include all kinds of snacks (especially chocolate), sparkly accessories, biking along Lake Michigan, and reading all kinds of stories—just not the fine print!

Sarah holds an MFA in Writing for Children and Young Adults from Vermont College of Fine Arts. She lives with her family in Evanston, Illinois. Find out more at www.sarah aronson.com.